my board of Salvation

Pamela in her quest for true love

For you who are going to read this book...

"The place where we place our eyes determines the direction of our lives."

I pray that this book inspires you to set your sight on the Master of our lives, Jesus. If Jesus is already your North, let Him revive in your heart the fire for serving Him.

With love,

Elia Jardo

Edited by Ofelia Pérez
Cover Art: Felix Gabriel Rodríguez
Interior design: Grupo Nivel Uno, Inc.
Cover photo: Dylan Rivera
Cover model: Rachelle Leduc

My Board of Salvation
Pamela in her quest for true love

ISBN: 978-1-7346498-2-6
www.elsailardo.com
www.mitabladesalvacion.com

Printed in the United States of America.
© 2020 by Hispanos Media

Enjoy your...
Board of *Salvation*

Elsa presents to us this singular novel, a story that resembles the lives of thousands of people and possibly reminds you what you have lived. I am sure you will enjoy going through these pages because they will allow you to reflect on the decisions you have made, the feelings you have, and you will ask yourself existential questions that we rarely ask ourselves. It is my wish that the novel will help many make wise decisions because the pain of bad decisions has a generational impact. Understanding why things happen to us, and how we get to where we are, is the mystery to solve. So, you will enjoy reading My Board of Salvation.

SIXTO PORRAS
Director of Focus on the Family for Iberoamérica

I am immensely happy about this extraordinary writing by my beloved friend Elsa! She pours her heart into everything she does, with brushstrokes of beauty and love. I am sure this project is no exception. God, in His infinite love, is in charge of raising people to remind us that even in the midst of life's crudest losses, childhood trauma, crisis, discouragement, heartbreak and incomprehensible situations, hope will always have room to flourish. The Holy Spirit will speak to you through each experience of Pamela. I invite you to read each line with depth and reflection. Her story will have similarities to yours, because her story contains pieces and canvases of what we have all experienced in this captivating adventure called life, in which we fall off cliffs, but we also find the ladder that takes us and leads us to the top. Just as Pamela discovered herself when she felt lost and was healed in the hands of the One who has the power to heal everything, you will also feel the bandages on your wounds in these pages that were fully revealed by God. Thank you, Elsa, for being brave and obedient to the voice of the Lord. This book is very necessary in the times in which we are living as a society. Anxiety disorders, depression and suicides have increased dramatically. I believe we will hear the testimonies of all those who through this reading will discover a way out of the labyrinth, to see light at the end of the tunnel and a real reason to shout: I found My Board of Salvation!

DRA. LIS MILLAND
Professional Counselor
International Speaker
Bestselling Author

A few years ago, God gave me the great privilege of meeting a person who later became a friend. She introduced me as an author in the beautiful world of literature; God used Elsa's life to open doors for me in the industry, and today I am excited to see that she is the one who takes a new step as an author. What a great joy! My first adventure on the paddle board was also with Elsa in Orlando. I remember that day we talked a lot about her project and the lessons that God was teaching her every time she practiced this beautiful sport. That impacted my life. Elsa is a wonderful woman. I admire her faith, trust, and passion for God. I have seen her fight and believe in the promises of God, and I know that this book you are reading was born in the heart of the Father and was placed in it to bring light and hope to many people who need to read this fascinating novel. I am sure that it will take you on a beautiful adventure that will not only delight you with reading, but in each experience you will be able to learn a lot from the revealed lessons, because there is only one salvation board for every life. Thank you, friend, for believing God and for being obedient to this new call. You have been trained for this and much more, so keep shining with the light of Jesus. Today I celebrate this first book, and I know that more will come.

Dear reader, open each page with faith, but above all, open your heart and receive the message of faith that is for you.

STEPHANIE CAMPOS

Author, Life Coach International Speaker

My Board of Salvation is a novel like no other. As you read each word, you will feel part of the story. You will laugh with the occurrences of the characters, but you will also cry and even relate with their decisions. If you have been in constant search of the love of your life, but you have not found it, *My Board of Salvation* will take you to Him. Elsa iLardo has written one of the best novels that you will read in your life.

SARINETTE CARABALLO PACHECO

Author of Dios en las redes sociales (God in Social Media)

John Maxwell Certified Coach and Founder

of ASK Leadership Team

Contemporary women are facing so many daily challenges. The story of many women today is related in such a descriptive way in this novel. *My Board of Salvation* will become one of the novels through which you can feel how God affirms you in different facets of your life. All of us at different times in our lives in one way or another will be faced with an opportunity where we will have to make the decision to manage our emotions and decisions at the height that God expects of us. The novel *My Board of Salvation* inspires us to be grounded in the Word of God and in a healthy relationship with Him. Thank you, Elsa, for such an exquisite reading. Dear reader, you will start the reading process assimilating the situation of many people. My expectation is that like the protagonists of this novel, you too will enjoy such a beautiful ending.

DAYNA MONTEAGUDO

Author of *Desde el corazón de una amiga*

(From the heart of a friend)

Meeting Elsa has been a great blessing. Her life has been a great and special example, an irreproachable testimony. When I had the opportunity to read this novel that will be known in the nations, I was identified because I know a God who restores and transforms like no one else. I did not doubt for a moment the blessing that will be for so many women. This is a novel that is needed at this time, and I have faith that it will impact nations. This novel is not just a story, but the right moment for you to identify yourself enough to find yourself and the purpose for which God created you. I know that we will hear for many generations of this beautiful story.

DR. RUTH MARÍ CALDERÓN

Author of *Mi altar sagrado*

The book *My Board of Salvation* is a fascinating novel that narrates a series of events that could have fatally marked the future of Pamela, the main character in the story. In each chapter the reader will feel identified with the events that occur during Pamela's life, stories of love, heartbreak, violence, and disappointment, among others. I highly recommend reading the book *My Board of Salvation*. It is a valuable resource for both women and men. The women will be able to identify with some of Pamela's seasons, and recognize if their lives are in the order that God yearns for. For men it is a reminder of how their actions can mark or bless the life of that lady they have as a life partner. My friend Elsa's book fills me with joy. This novel will be the beginning of a new season in her life and her family's. In the midst of the busy time we have to live, this book will be the board of salvation that many are waiting to bring their lives to the level of excellence that God has designed for each of their children.

TATIHANA POZO
Director of Media Group Context

In memory of someone *loved*

For almost 14 years, God allowed me to enjoy the company of a beautiful pet, a toy poodle that I named Penelope Sofía. Penelope came into our lives when I was a single mother of a 5-year-old boy, and seeking to give my son a little sister, I looked for the closest and most possible: a dog.

Very soon this little creature became part of my family. There was something special about her; it seemed that she perceived what I felt. I used to speak for her, creating her voice, and she acted exactly as if she understood. One day she escaped and got pregnant. When I realized her pregnancy, I jokingly told everyone that we were now the two single mothers. She had four puppies that were born in my blue truck while I was driving. What level of tension she made me live!

She moved from house to house with me, accompanied us through the worst crises; when we lost everything and when God provided for us again. I brought her with us to the United States, from one city to another. She was always my faithful dog. She had her little pink bed inside my room. She walked remarkably close behind me wherever I went; I did not need a "leash". She followed me close. There was no place for me to close the door and leave her outside; she cried until I opened it.

Near, happy and loving described her perfectly. With the ability to stand on two legs, turn and walk, all for a piece of meat or for the joy of seeing me arrive home. She used to run with me and seemed to smile. With the slightest gesture of affection, she threw herself on the floor waiting to be caressed. There is a character in this book that bears her name; that's how special Penelope was to me. Days after finishing writing this book, I went out to work and when I came back, Penelope was no longer alive. Penelope's life was violently taken away. Facing that hard shock during the joy of publishing this book was a whirlwind of emotions. The pain wanted to stop me from moving forward. I fell to my knees and cried out to heaven. Help could not come from anywhere else. But to get out of the emotional stagnation I was in, I needed to forgive. It is easy to preach forgiveness, but it is difficult to live what is preached. This seemed to be the last test before publishing *My Board of Salvation*. To do so, I needed to stop putting weight on "how it happened" and look with anticipation and joy "at what will happen"; set my sights on the things above and let God push me out of the pain zone. Some days it seemed simple, other days it seemed impossible. And just before this book came out, I went paddle boarding with my family.

We were in a river and there were fallen trees in the water. My children and my husband passed over them without problem and when I went to pass the keel of my board got stuck on the trunk and stopped me suddenly. This brought me to my knees, just as I fell at that terrible news. I tried with all my strength to push myself with the paddle, but it was impossible. My husband approached me and with tender patience and wisdom he explained: "You have to move the weight of your body to the front of the board; your weight is on the back and that's where the keel is". I must admit that I did not respond positively at first. Rather, I refused to continue; I backed away and became angry with life for having that trunk in my way. Actually, I felt sorry for myself; why do these things only happen to me? ... Hearing the sweet calls of my husband I went back ashamed. This time I decided to listen to his instructions and submit. When I moved forward, as he told me, the back of the board rose a little and I was able to break out of the stalemate. Yes, this was a wow moment!

What did God show me? That I cannot continue putting the weight in the past, on what happened. I need to move forward, to what continues, to the future, and only then I will be able to continue my journey. Things do not always happen as we would like, solutions are not always what we propose to God, tragedies happen, evil exists, and situations do not always seem fair. But we can focus on what is ahead and remove the weight from what has been left behind to continue advancing in the sea of life. Jesus said in John 16:33: "These things I have spoken to you so that in me you may have peace. In the world you will have affliction; but trust me, I have overcome the world".

Rest in peace, my cute little dog, thank you for your loyalty and for so many years of joy. I trust that when I arrive in heaven to meet Jesus, He will be carrying you on his side.

Dedication

I dedicate this book to my family.

To my mother, Elsa, for being a pillar in my life and an example of a strong and brave woman who struggled to support her children.

To my dad, who is in heaven; I know he would be proud of me.

To my brothers and sister, whom I love, David, Sonia, Junito, Eric and in heaven my "big-bro", José.

My son Dylan. With you I was not only a mom, but I became a better human being. You made me sensitive; you were the piece of the puzzle that God used to touch my heart. I did it for you and the prize was for me. Thank you for the young adult you have become; you make me so proud of you. Wise son and noble protector. Thank you for being so united with me. I love you so much, with all my heart.

And the God who gives out the multiplication must have been happy with me because through my husband he gave me another son, Cody. Thank you for loving and accepting me as your second mom. I love you and I am supremely proud of you, as much as I know that your beautiful mom will be in heaven. You draw a smile on my face with your sweetness and your big heart. I love you. Thank you for your help always and for giving me so much love.

To my husband Stephen, my best friend, my best complement. God was not wrong in uniting us. He brought you into my life, showed me your heart, and with each passing day I fall in love more. Thank you for taking care of me and for giving me so much love. Thank you for conquering me, for each day praying for me, for trying to understand my "English not very good looking". I love you, "mi-mor". With you until the end of our gray hair.

Jesus, if it were not for you, what would have become of me? You made me stop on the road, you saved me from death so many times, you rescued me from my bad decisions, you consoled me in sadness and you took me out of a thousand tribulations. You made me fall in love with you. You made me see that it was possible, you showed me the way, you taught me to wait and you gave me a great reward. Thanks for your rescue. You, without a doubt, are My Board of Salvation.

LET'S *start!*

Acknowledgments

From a young age I began to dream of writing. I still have my notebook of poems and writings that I started before I was 12 years old. All my life I dreamed for a day like today, but it would not have been possible if it were not for the key people that God put in my way so that this dream would become a reality.

One of those people is my editor, Ofelia Pérez. Thanks for believing in me. The books of great writers whom I admire have passed through your hands. I know first-hand how demanding you are with your job. I know very well how long you stop to correct every detail of a book that passes through your hands. For this reason, receiving a compliment from you is worth the United States lottery. Thank you for allowing yourself to be used by God to make this work possible.

Thanks also to my son Dylan, who was the cover photographer. and the beautiful model, Rachelle Leduc, who in a short time has won my heart and love. To Gabriel Rodríguez, the graphic designer; managing to capture the essence of what was in my mind and heart was not an easy task, and you did it. I must thank my number one fanatic, my husband Stephen, who propelled me, motivated me, and inspired me to continue even during the worst storm. Having a family that is also my team is a blessing.

In my walk, which was designed by hand by God, I had the opportunity to work with a Christian publisher. Being part of that company was the excuse that God used to put in my way people who would impact my life forever. Some of the people who were my coworkers are still my brothers and sisters. Tony, Brenda, and Marilyn, thank you for your advice, your help, and for joining me in the process.

I also want to thank author José Luis Navajo. I cannot call him José Luis, nor can I call him Navajo. From the day I met him I called him "Pastor". He and his wife Gene have molded me with their example and their beautiful love. Your daily life reflects integrity. Noting the beautiful value, he places on his wife, daughters, and grandchildren has been inspiring for my husband and me. It is an honor to have a foreword written by you. Thank you for inspiring me, for your advice and for hugging me like a daughter. My family and I are eternally grateful for your life.

There was another person who played a fundamental role for me. Meeting Sixto Porras, Director of Focus on the Family for Ibero-America, was another great blessing from heaven. He was a great teacher and counselor when I was faced with the struggles of being a single mother. On one occasion I took my son for a work trip where I oversaw Don

Sixto's schedule. His attentions to my son and his affection were engraved in my heart. Sixto is always the same, a heart filled with the love of Christ.

I also want to thank my beloved friend, Dr. Lis Milland, another person that God intentionally chose to cross my path. She has been a great blessing to my family. You were there for me and you extended your heart to my brother, my mom and even my best friend. There is no doubt that you will find the advice I received from you in this book through Dr. Lisa. How much I have learned with you and how much I enjoy you! Thank you!

To my four author friends:

Dayna Monteagudo, always ready for giving me timely advice; you did not let me delay this book.

Sarinette Caraballo, a heart full of gold ideas, thanks for inspiring me to do more, always more.

Dr. Ruth Calderón, I met you in a "sudden" and you disappear and appear, but you always arrive full of blessing and inspiration.

To my little sister, Stephanie Campos, life has allowed us to be always united and shaking hands, me for you and you for me. Let us keep building together.

Each of you served as inspiration.

Two friends who have never left me regardless of distance.

My beloved Limaris: there is never a "no" for me; you are always there.

My beloved friend Jonathan, whom God used in my most difficult season.

My gratitude for you is eternal.

And finally, I thank my mom for her unconditional support and for believing in me. Thank you for raising my arms and not only being my mother, but also my friend. I love you.

Thank you, God, for dictating this book to my heart. I recognize that all the glory is for You and that if a life is transformed by the letters shared here it is because your Holy Spirit knows for whom they were written. Thank you for entrusting me with this great treasure, My Board of Salvation.

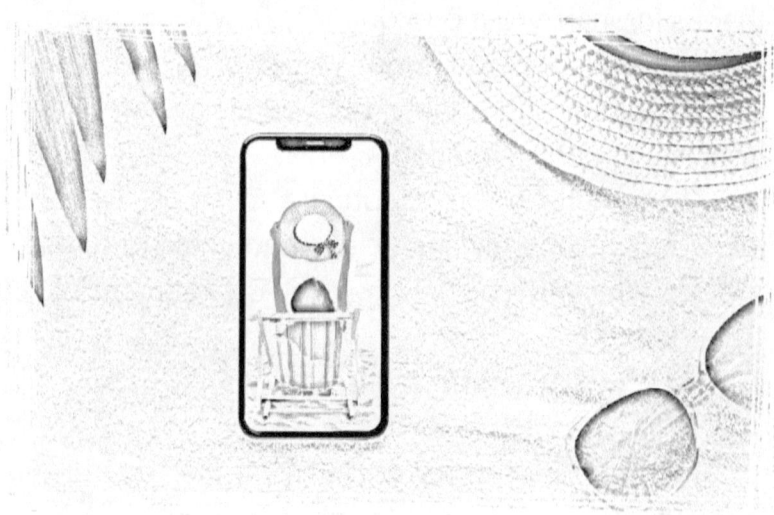

Table of contents

Foreword

There are writers who do not write sentences, but paint pictures.

Each phrase is an image that invites you to dive. The way they immerse the reader in the story is comparable to diving in a sea of letters and discovering treasures in the depths of that ocean of ink.

Something like this happens with *My Board of Salvation*. It is a realistic novel that wraps us in a hug that at times is freezing but ends up being a healing therapy.

Pamela's story is that of thousands, perhaps millions of people who do not claim more, but not less, than to find true love. In her complicated journey she is suffering disappointments; each one of them is a tear in Pamela's soul.

Disappointment after disappointment is plunging her into a deeper and deeper abyss.

It is then that she learns a lesson: when you reach the bottom, you must lean on Jesus to jump.

Everything seems lost, but ... on the fourth watch of the darkest night she finally finds the Ruin Restorer.

To the blessed Scribe who writes perfect lines on crooked lines. To the divine craftsman who takes the rubble that others left and turns them into a palace.

God sutures Pamela's wounds with gold thread and turns them into wealth.

Prepare the reader to get excited in reading; maybe you even break. Remember then that the tears shed for just causes clarify our vision and become irrigation water that provides an explosion of life.

I think Pamela will mark hearts with the story of her life. It will leave traces on which many will tread and will light a thousand lights in the downcast spirit.

Thank you, Elsa, for this wonderful legacy that you leave us. May God be the first of many to fill the soul of your readers with oxygen.

Without further ado, ladies, and gentlemen, relax, find a quiet space, and welcome to a journey that will not leave anyone indifferent: MY BOARD OF SALVATION!

Jose Luis Navajo
Author of *Lunes con mi viejo pastor* (Monday with My Old Shepherd) and over 20 bestsellers

Introduction

I open my eyes to a new reality. He is gone.

My God, tell me, is this the end? He has come in and out of my life so many times. I fear for my life. Please, God, promise me you will take care of me.

I get up from the couch dazed. I spent the night on the mattress trying not to fall asleep to make sure that he would not break the door. I run to my daughter Penelope's room and she is asleep. How could she not notice anything?

I go to the closet, and his clothes are gone, also his suitcase, his drawers are empty. I run to the attic and his gun is still there. I think it is time to run away from here.

A note on our bed stops me. I do not know whether to open it or leave it closed. But I need to know, what is going to happen? Is this the end?

The note says: "Pamela, I will always love you. Forgive me for not knowing how to love you. This experience was too much for me. Now I am the one who does not want to see you again. God loves you; I have never felt anything like this. I was not sure if He was real. Now I know He is. Stay with God, with your daughter and with your life. This is not for me. If I stay here, I might end up killing you. Tomorrow I will file for divorce. I am going to Mexico; I do not want to be here anymore. I did not deserve what you did to me. Manuel."

What I did to him? That is nervy.

Last night he walked through the door so drunk that I thought he was going to kill me. We have been separated for three months and he wants to continue in his habits, his mistreatment, his abandonment, his abuses, his women and that I serve him as a slave to his cravings.

I said no and ran out of the room. He ran after me saying horrible things. He took me by the neck as he threatened me, and I was only crying out to heaven for God's help. His eyes widened as if he had seen hell itself. He released me and looked at me with dread in his eyes.

-Who are you? - he asked.

I replied: - What's wrong with you? I am Pamela.

-Shut up, get out of my life. Do not talk to me anymore, do me a favor, do not touch me - he said, screaming.

I did not understand anything that was happening. He had a dazed look in his eyes; they were red, he looked like he was tormented.

-Well, I do not know if you speak to God or the devil, but he spoke to me. And he said if I touch you, I will die. I heard it. Didn't you hear him?

- No, Manuel, but what you felt was the fear of God. Do not hurt me anymore please, get out of here - I begged him.

He fell to his knees in an uncontrolled cry. I do not know how my daughter did not wake up. I sat on the sofa terrified; I did not know what to expect next. He seemed insane. He started to crawl on four legs and went to the bedroom. It sounded as if he was packing, but I did not dare get close to him.

I just prayed: - Lord, take care of our lives, Father. I kept my eyes closed, crying, and I could not stop praying. Maybe ten minutes passed and suddenly the door slammed. He left the house. I heard his Porsche's engine start and go full speed. I cried out to God giving thanks.

-Lord, I am alive, Father, you have saved me once again.

-I began to stack furniture against the door so that he could not get back inside. A mixture of joy and fear invaded me. Peace and uncertainty at the same time. I went back to the couch to continue praying, asking that he did not come back. "I will wait until dawn and I will go to my mom's house; I will never return to this place", I said to myself.

Oh my God, I spent the night on that couch. The nightmare ended. A text message pops up my cell phone, it is Manuel. It cannot be. Fear invades me again. The text includes two photos. The photo of his plane ticket to Mexico and the photo of the divorce petition. "Goodbye, Pamela, I don't want to see you again."

I felt peace. I felt pain.

Manuel used his contacts and influences to have in his hand an application to initiate the divorce in just a few hours. Money was not an obstacle for him, I suppose he paid a high price for that airfare. What will happen to his life and his businesses? I do not know, and I really do not want to know.

I prayed ...

Lord, why am I in this situation? I thought I had been married for life.

I thought you would solve it.

-Daughter...read 2 Timothy 3: 2-5 and you will find answers.

For people will love only themselves and their money. They will be boastful and proud, scoffing at God, disobedient to their parents, and ungrateful. They will be unloving and unforgiving; they will slander others and have no self-control. They will be cruel and hate what is good. They will betray their friends, be reckless, be puffed up with pride, and love pleasure rather than God. They will act religious, but they will reject the power that could make them godly. Stay away from people like that!

Peace.

- Lord, I am 28 years old and have made so many mistakes in my life. Is it possible that you will change my situation? Will it be possible for you?

"I am the Lord, the God of all the peoples of the world. Is anything too hard for me?"
(Jeremiah 32:27)

"For the word of God will never fail."
(Luke 1:37)

Chapter

1

Stand over the *Sea*

"The safest place to fall is on your knees."

Elia Jardo

I could not believe this was happening. It had been a beautiful wedding on a beach like this... close friends, a romantic rain, which, now that I think about it, seemed to forecast that it would be a marriage full of tears... but I thought it was the hallmark of our love. It had been one month since we divorced, and it was necessary to put a stop to it. Having a few days alone to think, to relax in another country, should do me good. At least that is what my friend-psychologist Lisa said.

I find myself on a beautiful beach in Aruba, completely alone, trying to put together the broken pieces that remained of a frustrated marriage full of yelling, mistreatment, abuse, and intimidation. I had only known the unexpected.

Here in Aruba I do not know anyone. I need to take a few days and think. My daughter stayed with my mom in Miami. My counselor says I need time to heal, my pastor says I need God to heal me. Time... God... Heal? Both agree that I need to heal because I am sick (she says), broken (says he), crazy (I say)! Yes, crazy, because it seems that I have made the wrong choice many times. I am 28 years old, I am a single mother, divorced from a failed stepfather and abandoned many times. Could it be I am the problem?

So, well, here I am in this paradisiacal place. I must do something fun, something I have always wanted to do, but yet, I have never dared. I would love to paddleboard! I must keep myself happy, I cannot allow myself to become depressed and, on that note, He clearly told me: something better is yet to come. I must believe. I will need to read that letter every day until I can believe it. A six-page letter that marked my life.

I will walk down to the beach and see if I find one of those places that rents equipment and trains people. How ironic that I am alone in this beautiful place. Perhaps here I will find true love...

- Calm down, Pamela, calm down, focus, and do not look around. You do not need to contact the first lifeguard that crosses your path. - I thought.

Uh! I can see a little man with the boards, that is, they are renting the equipment. I went over to ask.

- How much is it to rent a paddleboard? - I asked in Spanish because he had a Latino face.

- They are $25 for an hour if you have experience. If you have not done it before, I must go with you and train you, and that costs $35 an hour. Do you have experience? - asked the man.

For a moment I confess that my thought was to lie. I wanted to, but I did not want to pay extra for my lack of experience.

-Is that the price for my ignorance? - I asked sarcastically.

He nodded as he said: "People die in the water due to lack of experience and knowledge".

Ugh! The concept has never been so clear to me until that day: *"My people are destroyed for lack of knowledge"* (Hosea 4:6 NASB). I think God is speaking to me, I thought.

So, determined to embark on this new experience, I paid the price.

After a boring training on the sand that I thought I did not need, we entered the water and he indicated that I should start kneeling.

I looked around and saw other people entering the water and standing directly on the paddleboard, so I decided not to follow the advice and said:

- No, let us go straight to the action, I want to learn standing up at once. -He nodded his head in ironic bewilderment and allowed me to begin my adventure. I stood on the board and my knees started shaking immediately.

I was completely exposed to all the people on that beach and had no idea what the next step was. And I remembered an important detail; I only learned how to doggie paddle; that is, I do not know how to swim!

There I was, standing on the board and stunned. It was my decision, but from that moment I knew that I should follow his advice and start on my knees. But, let us be brave, we are here.

- What is the next step? I asked, pretending to be in control.

- You need to start moving. - His ironic tone was evident.

- You must do what I told you on the shore. Remember? - I had been giving him attitude throughout the lesson and apparently, he realized it.

- You must keep paddling, stay on the center of the paddleboard, and do not lose balance so you do not fall. - He explained patiently.

While we were on the sand, he gave me a comprehensive explanation of what to do in the water. We even did exercises on the sand on how to perform. Honestly, I looked down on that time, realizing I did not give him all my attention and was already sorry I had not listened better. Pride was stronger. I did not want to feel like a novice in front of so many people, come on! At that moment, my life began to go through my head like a movie. I began to remember how many times the pastor, my mom, and my closest friends wanted to warn me about what marriage was like, and the reasons why I should at least consider the possibility that he was not the one. But I did not listen. Just as I did not consider the fact of not knowing how to swim to decide to try paddle boarding and I did not want to put on my life jacket. I came to marriage just as I came to this paddleboard, without having prepared myself enough, without wanting to listen and receive advice and without knowing what the right thing was to do. I did not listen. But, well, let us start paddling. At last we are here.

I began to move slowly, and amid my fear it was nice to hear people speaking Spanish in the water and being above the sea you hear everything. Even the laughter when someone on another paddleboard fell into the water, how cruel!

- Vea, mae, no sabés lo que estás haciendo—*

That was the comment that brought me closer. The accent was "pura vida"** in my ears. A group from Costa Rica that was on vacation. I approached with my paddle board trying to look confident and smiling, but in truth, I was looking for an excuse to stop. So, I asked them:

- Have you done this before? - But I could not hear the answer because at that moment I lost my balance, and while I wobbled and felt like a moron, I only managed to listen ...

- Drop to your knees - It was the voice of my coach who knew I was about to fall into the sea. And without hesitation for a moment I did. I threw myself on my knees on the board; it was impressive to realize

---

* - See, Mae, you do not know what you are doing –
** pure life

the power of that action. That move prevented my fall; I could hardly believe it.

> "Daughter, the *safest place* to fall is on your knees."

I heard a sweet voice in my heart. What do you want to teach me? I know you are here today. It was the voice of God.

I was on the paddleboard on my knees and at that moment I decided it was time to take a break, and I sat on my paddleboard to talk to my new friends, who would not stop laughing, while the rental clock kept ticking. I swallowed my shame because the fear of standing up was greater. That time helped me a little to calm my nerves, just like my vacation in Aruba was doing.

- Where are you from? - They asked me.

- I am from a nice little town on the west coast of Puerto Rico-. I replied. And how could I not see what was coming next?

- But if you are from Puerto Rico you must be an expert in surfing and paddleboarding - commented one of them. People think that if you are from an island you automatically know how to swim, fish, and have a boat. But, anyway, I got distracted for a while until I gained courage and decided to return to reality. The coach waited silently, looking at the clock.

So, I said to myself, "I just have to do exactly what I did in the beginning to stand on the board". But something happened. I completely lost my balance and without knowing how to regain it, in my process of stopping, I fell into the sea mercilessly. I have to say that I am grateful that I did not hit my head on the board, that would have been terrible. At that moment, my nerves took over, I thought I was going to drown, I did not know how to swim, so as soon as possible, I held the board with one hand. I was so nervous about drowning that I could not hear what people around me were saying:

- It is only four feet deep, put your feet on the sand.

-My feet on the sand? I did not know what was worse; the shame of having fallen or of thinking that I was drowning. And it is that amid any situation, our concern for our image is a lethal weapon to place shame on us.

I was a single mother at just 18 years old. My daughter, Penelope Sofía, is 10 today, she is my greatest pride. Her name Penelope means "the one who waits" and her name Sofia means "wisdom". Exactly what I needed: knowing how to wait and wisdom.

There were many times that I was pointed out for not having acted in the right manner. No one seemed to demand the same from the father of my daughter who had gone to conquer other women, leaving me pregnant, while I had to face the world.

- Pamela, come back to the paddleboard, nothing happens - the coach told me patiently with his Venezuelan accent. Just like when we fail and that good Shepherd tells

"The *life-jacket* prevents the ascent."

us, nothing happens, daughter, come on Sunday. But I thought to myself: "I'm going to surprise the coach; I won't wait for him to recommend I use the life jacket". So, I untied it from the board and while in the water, I put it on. The coach looked at me with a surprised face and smiled. I thought I was showing off. I buttoned all the buttons and said, "Done, I'm going to get on the board". Now I was determined to learn and take it seriously. But it was impossible to get on the board. The life jacket would not let me. It was a hindrance. At that moment I hear the coach's voice, subtly say ...

-Child, that life jacket is going to make it impossible for you to achieve what you set out to do. Take off your life jacket if you want to climb. –

It was a Whoa! moment for me. I wondered: how many other life jackets have been taking me away from my destiny? I had looked at men like a life jacket. That is what my therapist Lisa said. I was always in a hurry to meet the love of my life. I felt that I was getting older, that perhaps no one would love me, that I did not deserve to be happy ... So, my fears led me to seek for a life jacket, but that life jacket was hindering my climb to the paddleboard, so, be gone!

"My *Power* is perfected in your weakness."

I took off my life jacket and used all my strength to climb onto the board. But my arms did not help me do it. They were not holding me. I have never been strong in the upper part of my body, and the gym and I are fighting. I looked at the sky asking: how can I do it with my own strength, I cannot?

I could feel an answer in my heart that told me: - My power is perfected in your weakness -. That voice, again ... It was not the first time I heard it, but I began to discern it every day. It was not always clear to me. I had accepted Jesus in my heart, but I did not give Him the Lordship over my life. I wanted it to be a leisurely relationship. At that time "my instinct" told me that if I put one leg on the board, since my legs were stronger than my arms, maybe that would help me raise half of my body and my arms would only have to raise the other part. So, I did, I placed one leg on the board and the rest of my body came with it. The power to discover where your strength lies is wonderful. So, there I was back on the paddleboard, but this time on my knees, humble. I looked at the coach and said: - Now I want to get it right, what am I supposed to do? - In this process I was able to realize that my impulses are not going to take me as far as my patience can take me in the process.

I thought: "Sometimes life gives us second chances". My mother often says that sometimes falling is an act of God's mercy to avoid a greater and an eternal fatality. I cannot deny that those moments help us open our eyes and realize

> "Sometimes falling is an act of God's *mercy* to avoid a greater and an eternal fatality."

how much more we need to learn. So, I decided to start again, and the coach said to me:

- You already know how to stop; apply what you have learned. - It seemed that every lesson the coach gave me was a blow to the reality of my life. I stood up, because I had already fallen so many times in my life that I knew exactly that the next step was simply to stand up without much thought. And I started doing what I already knew as well: paddle, push forward.

Who REMAINS ON HIS *knees,* hardly falls.

It is on
OUR KNEES that we
get strong
and become
wise.

Chapter
2

Deep lessons

"In order to move forward we have to dig deep"

Elisa Isando

"It is hard for you to kick against the goads".

(ACTS 26:14 NASB)

"Pamela, I want to explain something to you, and I want you to please pay attention to me." I felt scolded, but I humbly accepted it because there was really so much sweetness in his voice. "I have been practicing water sports for many years, I am from the island of Margarita in Venezuela. By the way, you can call me Luis", he said smiling. - If I had children, they would be your age, but my good God did not grant my wife and I that great privilege. He gave us many others, and many spiritual children.

-His remark put an automatic lump in my throat. I lost my dad at 5 and to this day I remember him as my superhero that I have never stopped missing. I am "Daddy's Little Girl" - that is what he called me. I wanted to hug him in that instant. But I held myself back.

> "Losing your calm takes you to dangerous extremes, and losing your *balance* anticipates a fall."

- The teachings you are going to receive, you will be able to apply them in the water, but they will also be great life lessons. - He continued explaining patiently.

-Let's talk about balance and calm. Balance: you need to stay in the center. If you go to extremes, your weight will make you lose balance and losing balance is the down payment on falling. Calm: when you lose your calm, you make mistakes and unconsciously push your body to extremes, which will make you lose balance and fall. So, do not get out of the center or lose your cool. -

Whoa! You are right, I need to apply this in life. Every time I get "extreme" I get into trouble, and every time I lose my calm, I put my feet in it.

-Luis continued explaining: - To achieve these two basic principles, you must practice in safe situations. Do not expose yourself before you are ready. So, I want you to go from point A to point B for a good time so that you become familiar with your board and the sea. I want you to stay in this sector that I am pointing out because whatever happens, you can hear my voice and you are in shallow depth. –

That was a tremendous idea. He set clear limits for me and instructed me to familiarize myself before committing. I should have known that before I got married. I started paddling from one point to the other. Each repetition gave me more confidence in what I was doing. I started to feel comfortable. After a while, my comfort was so great that I felt joy! In the church that I attend they sing a Colombian song that began to come out of me: "I will not go back, always forward I will go, I came to conquer the land that you give me, and like Joshua, your Word I will keep, and like Joshua, you called me to conquer". This started to be therapeutic, great! I felt like a surfer in Aruba.

I meditated on everything that was happening on the other side of the world. I reviewed the decisions I had to make and confronted my deepest fears. After months of darkness I felt alive again. Honestly, I did not feel pain for divorcing him, I felt a lot of regret for marrying him. I knew everything was going to be better now, but I also knew it was a process.

> "Get familiar before committing."

> "Lord, I want to let the force of your presence move me, that the bravery of your love defend me, that the experience of your eternity guide me."

Little by little, I gained confidence with the board until I decided that I wanted to move forward, take speed. I wanted to impress, but the truth is that my arms were burning, and it was not from the sun. I felt that I had no strength. I hit the water trying to go fast.

At the distance, the coach seemed to notice my fight and with a soft voice he said to me:

-Don't fight with the sea. He is stronger than you, braver and more experienced. Use your strength to flow with it. –

Whoa! I said out loud. This is God, this is my life. I keep fighting to move forward. Fighting in my strength to change what I cannot and to go at my own pace. *"O people of Israel, do not fight against the Lord, the God of your ancestors, for you will not succeed!"* (2 Chronicles 13:12)

At that moment I prayed: "Lord, I want to let the force of your presence move me, that the bravery of your love defend me, that the experience of your eternity guide me."

I want to flow with his Spirit, as others do. I want to stop trying to help you. I think God can do everything without me. I wanted to control everything that happens in my life, and who controls the sea? Only God. I have not known how to enjoy good times and learn to wait in difficult times. I did not want to know the seasons and recognize if the winds are favorable or contrary. I have spent my life fighting with the sea. Whipping it to advance. How different would it be if

I calm down if I leave the rush out? Each teaching was awakening within me. *"For everything there is a season, a time for every activity under heaven:* (Ecclesiastes 3:1)

"Vanity of vanities, says the Preacher, vanity of vanities! All is vanity. What advantage does man have in all his work. Which he does under the sun? (Ecclesiastes 1:2-3, NASB)

After that deep meditation, I felt ready enough to get out of that limited space that the coach had given me. So, I asked him:

- Can I move to other waters? And he said to me:

-If you feel confident, do it, but remember, if you want to advance, you must go deep with the paddle.

I promise you; I did not understand what he was saying. I think he expected me to ask him, but for honor and dignity (pride), I made myself like I understood. Very soon he would find out. I started paddling around the beach. I got quite close to the shore and then moved away from the shore ... And I do not know at what point I went to an area that was considered open sea, that is, more than 10 feet deep perhaps ... I realized because I began to see the boats passed remarkably close to me, and the jet-skis were almost flying. The waves were starting to get higher and higher, and it was very intimidating. I have no idea how deep the sea could be, but my heart began to pound at 1,000 miles per hour. I cried

"Who remains on his *knees,* hardly falls."

out to God and thought: "I did not come to Aruba to die; Lord, help me. " It was so far away that I couldn't hear the coach's voice and on top of it I had my back to the shore. We had not gotten to the turning around lesson. All I could think about was getting down on my knees and praying at once. I remembered that the one who remains on his knees, hardly falls. In doing so, I felt that I was taking control of the situation a bit.

"In order to move forward, we have *to dig* deep."

It seemed peculiar to me that we had not talked about how to rotate the board 180 degrees. Just as perhaps the coach found it peculiar that I had gotten into this problem at sea. I had to let go of instinct, which was the voice of God in my heart. Little by little I managed to turn the paddleboard towards the shore. As I did so I could tell that the coach was raising his arms trying to tell me something.

Sometimes we get so far away that we stop listening to the voice that directs us. We isolate ourselves from our family and from the people who love us and seek to guide us. That is exactly what I did. I isolated myself from my church, my pastors, my family, and my friends by entering a marriage that was like a dangerous open sea full of sharks. But I said to myself, "This is not the time to think about it, it is the time to think about the solution." And I remembered the last words the coach had said to me: "If you want to advance, you have to go deep with the paddle". In faith, without understanding, I did it.

"Daughter, to be able to advance, dig deep."

I started to put the paddle into the sea as deep as I could. Being on my knees I felt safe and felt I had better control. I focused on paddling and put my gaze and my total concentration on what I was doing. As I did, I imagined that each paddle was a cry to God. I was able to understand that when we are in a dangerous situation, we only move forward when we deeply meddle with the Lord.

I had avoided going into the depths and at that moment I understood that I was only going to be able to advance if I began to go deep into the understanding of His Word, deepening my prayers and my relationship with Him. It was not long before I was in front of the coach. And with a smile of approval he greeted me. How good it feels when you have made so many mistakes and still, there is someone who can smile and say, "well done". When there is someone who can look at your effort and recognize that although you have been wrong, you have struggled to get ahead of the situation.

I was exhausted. It was time to go to the room and rest. I had done the full month's exercise in one afternoon. And I had learned so much. I had a lot to ponder ...

blog

Hello friends, today I start an adventure: my blog, My lifeline. I have decided to open a page where I will share my paddle board learning process. Follow my adventures. Today I will start by sharing what I learned.

My 12 lessons from my first day on the board:

- Listen to the instructions while you are out of the water. There is no reason to learn from mistakes.
- Be humble; you always start on your knees. Who is in a hurry?
- Keep your center. If you go to extremes, you lose balance and fall.
- Use the life jacket before, not when you are already in trouble.
- Sometimes the life jacket hinders the climb plan.
- If you are going to fall, drop to your knees. He who remains on his knees hardly falls.
- Don't let shame damage life's adventure.
- Discover where God put your strengths and use them to propel you.
- Stay calm in times of crisis or you will fall precipitously.

- Set clear limits and familiarize yourself before committing.
- Don't fight with the sea. Enjoy the ride and the process.
- Go deeper when you want to advance. It is not about going fast, but deep. "Listen to counsel and accept discipline, that you may be wise the rest of your days"(Proverbs 19:20, NASB)

If you liked it, share it on your social networks and use #Myboardofsalvation

 SHARE

Even with **SCARS** and **WOUNDS,** I must continue and *walk* on the water.

Chapter
3

A new
beginning

"For I am about to do something new. See, I have already begun! Do you not see it? I will make a pathway through the wilderness. I will create rivers in the dry wasteland."

(ISAIAH 43:19)

What a thrill, I finally started my own blog! I had always wanted to. This is truly a new beginning. I feel so happy!

I cannot stop my thoughts about everything learned this afternoon. How many times in life have I entered situations without knowing what I was getting into? What guts of mine! I wonder, why do I always have to make mistakes first and then learn the lesson? Why can't I learn first so I do not make the mistake? I hope my mother is not listening because she would have a lot to say about it.

As I reflect on all the impulsive moments in my life, I must admit that I have spent my entire life looking for a man to fill the emptiness that was inside my heart. I had never stopped to think about whether I am ready to enter a relationship until Lisa, my therapist told me. The emptiness left by my father's death was evident. I remember him big, strong, so handsome, brave, and loving. Every day of my life I have missed him. I remember when we played on the beach, when he tickled me and my mother, the walks on his shoulders, my joy when he got home. I remember perfectly.

One day he went out fishing and never came back. His body was never found, the sea swallowed him up. So many fears that arose in me from that! Since then I had decided to contemplate the sea from the shore. It was a feeling of intimidation that paralyzed me. Today was a day of conquest. My daughter, Penelope Sofia, on the other hand, was a little fish in the sea. From a young age I began to bring her to the beach and through it I was able to make peace with the sea. Today was a great day. There is no doubt that something new began today.

I left the room to look for some ice and as I tried to return to the room, the key magnet had stopped working. Why does that always happen to me? Is it just me? I went down to the lobby to ask the girl at the reception area to change my key and while I was waiting, I heard a sweet female voice with a Venezuelan accent close to me. I turned to look, and she was a truly short woman of about 55+ years old in her hotel maid uniform. I was so happy when I heard Spanish! There is nothing better than listening to someone speaking your language when you are in a strange country. So, I did not hesitate to go meet her.

- Hola, mi nombre es Pamela,* do you work here? -

The question was obvious, but it was an excuse to start the conversation. And with such a motherly tone that I thought I was hearing my real mom, she replied: - Si, mi hermosa niña,** here for anything you need. - she told me.

I could not resist giving her a happy hug. I felt vulnerable and her sweet tone at the time was like the Bible says, health to my bones. *"Pleasant words are a honeycomb, sweet to the soul and healing to the bones"* (Proverbs 16:24, NASB).

> "Pleasant words are a honeycomb, sweet to the soul and healing to the bones."
>
> (Proverbs 16:24, NASB).

- My name is Pamela, and I am here on vacation, I live in Miami. What is your name? - My name is Sandra, I am a native of Maracaibo, but I lived many years in Margarita and my husband and I came to Aruba 3 years ago, we are waiting for some documents to go live in Miami soon. - She commented enthusiastically. - We are going to live there with my husband's brother to help him with his business. So, now we are both working here in Aruba. I am a waitress here in

---

*. Hello, my name is Pamela
**. Yes, my beautiful girl

the hotel restaurants and my husband has a paddle board business on the beach - she commented. Do not tell me! - I exclaimed surprised. - Is your husband a short chunky one? - I asked. "Yes," she replied, "his name is Luis," he said. – Whoa! how small is the world. If it is him, I was his student at the beach today. - We both laugh at the great coincidence. It was a peculiar coincidence. I already knew that the island is tiny, but here I understood the saying that "Boy it's a small world".

Sandra was the wife of my paddle board coach. I felt such a special connection to this woman, as if I had known her for a lifetime. I felt like she was my family, I wanted to hug her again and again. At that moment, the girl with my new card interrupted to give it to me and Sandra went to take an order from some people in the lobby. "I have to talk to her again," I said to myself. So, I patiently waited and walked over to her when she was done, and I said, Sandra, thanks. Thanks for what girl? Just knowing you makes me feel safe. I feel like I am not alone here in Aruba. I struggle with anxieties and coming alone on vacation to this country has been a challenge. No, my girl, you are not alone. You have a Heavenly Father who always takes care of you, and He places people like us close to what you need.

- You do not know how much I learned today with your husband; it really was a blessing for me. I commented. She said to me, look, let us do something. I finish my shift today at 8:00 pm. Go take a shower, rest, and catch me here in the lobby at that hour. My husband and I are going to take a walk around the city. You can come with us. We do not have physical children, but we do have many spiritual children that God has allowed us to care for in times of need, and we have room for another daughter. Her words filled my eyes with tears of emotion. She did not know that her husband had said something exactly like that to me and she was opening a door that was very desirable to me: spiritual parents. How nice it is to find people like that on the road! They are like a gift to the distressed soul.- It is a deal Sandra, see you here at 8:00. -

I went happily to my room, knowing that the damaged card was just an excuse from God to allow me to have this moment. I just met her, and I felt that she was family, sent, I do not know, something almost supernatural, I thought. And then she is the coach's wife, this is getting good. I am not alone anymore!

It was 5:00 in the afternoon, I sat for a while on the balcony of my room to watch the sunset. I love the sunsets. Sunset is the promise of tomorrow, and it comes with an invitation to rest in God. I must begin the assignment that my psychologist Lisa had recommended to me. I had to make a list of the negative thoughts that came to my mind and caused me sadness and put a verse from the Word of God

> "Sunset is the *promise* of tomorrow, and it comes with an invitation to rest in God."

to cancel them. Finding a Christian psychologist was another direct send from God into my life. Lisa was from Argentina and the afternoons of meeting with her were crazy between learning and laughter. What a charming personality that woman had! She was the one who inspired me to write all the memories as they happened and motivated me to start my own blog. But that list ... that list was confrontational.

This is my list of destructive thoughts that I must replace:

- I am completely alone.
- I have been overlooked.
- Nobody needs me.
- I do not matter.
- Nobody cares what happens to me.
- He will not return.
- God has also abandoned me.
- There is no one to protect me.
- I cannot trust anyone.
- I am afraid that they will not come back, or lose them.

What a terrible list! Seeing it in front of me broke my spirit. But immediately the voice of God came to rescue me. And once again he began to whisper in my ear, and I began to write his voice.

- I am not alone because Matthew 28:20 (NASB) says: "I am with you always, even to the end of the age."
- God never overlooks me because His Word says: "Look at the birds. They do not plant or harvest or store food in barns, for your heavenly Father feeds them. And aren't you far more valuable to him than they are? (Matthew 6:26)
- I am important because God says: "Others were given in exchange for you. I traded their lives for yours because you are precious to me. You are honored, and I love you." (Isaiah 43:4)
- I am valuable because God says: "She is more precious than rubies" (Proverbs 31:10)
- God is interested in what happens to me and He says: "What is the price of five sparrows, two copper coins? Yet God does not forget one of them. And the very hairs on your head are all numbered. So, don't be afraid; you are more valuable to God than a whole flock of sparrows." (Luke 12:6-7)
- Even if they do not come back ... "Even if my father and mother abandon me, the LORD will hold me close." (Psalm 27:10)
- God never abandons me... "When you pass through the waters, I will be with you; and through the rivers, they will overflow you. When you walk through the fire, you will not be scorched, nor will the flame burn you." (Isaiah 43:2, NASB)

- I am protected by Him ... "God is our refuge and strength, always ready to help in times of trouble." (Psalm 46:1)
- I trust ... "But when I am afraid, I will put my trust in you." (Psalms 56:3)
- I will not fear ... "The Lord himself will fight for you. Just stay calm." (Exodus 14:14)

I will use this list on my blog. If you help me, you can help other people. #Myboardofsalvation

4

Advises to the *soul*

Do not seek a new beginning in the heart,
but in the spirit. Fall in love with God.

Elsa Hardo

*"That which is born of the flesh is flesh; and
that which is born of the Spirit is spirit.*

(JOHN 3:6, NASB)

The afternoon had fallen, and I got up to relax a little after that mental exercise. I knew it was a necessary process to heal, but it was also intense. Like my therapist Lisa told me. While taking a refreshing bath I thought: "How could I make so many mistakes? Why do I always make wrong decisions? I have been a terrible example for my daughter, Penelope. But hey, there is nothing to regret. I am here to start again, and I will live the process until I heal."

I rested a little and got up ready to go to discover Aruba with my new friends. I could not see them among the people in the lobby, so I went to a small cafe in the hotel overlooking the beautiful Caribbean Sea. It was starting to get dark out, but the breeze and the sound of the sea were a gift from God. I asked for a lemonade while I waited and meditated on that verse that says: "So it is good to wait quietly for salvation from the Lord" (Lamentations 3:26). I have learned that when I am quiet, I save time and when I wait, I get a reward. I will not anticipate God's plans for my life, because He has a plan and I want to know Him.

> "When I am quiet, I save time and when I wait, I get a *reward.*"

My face lit up when I saw Sandra's smile approaching, sweet and bright. How are you Miss I wondered? Sandra, what a joy to see you again, but I am not a Miss, I am a Mrs. Ah, well, in that case you must be happy with your husband. Where is the lucky one? Well, that is a long story that maybe I will tell you later I replied. Ok, we will have time for that. I finished my workday for today and my husband and I want to invite you to visit Aruba.

I wanted with all my heart to get out of the hotel and get to know other areas, but I had no one with whom to go. So, going for a walk with two people who speak my language was wonderful. Sandra and I walked outside and Luis, the coach, was waiting for us there. Hello, Don Luis, how are you? Casually, today I met your wife. Yes, yes, Sandra told me that you met, but can you remove the "Don", which makes me older.

We all laughed. Ok, Luis. And how did I do today in the paddleboard? It was my first time, it was not too bad, I think. - Luis nodded gently and then said: You just must learn to let yourself be led by the one who knows. If you listen and let yourself be guided by someone else's wisdom and experience, everything will go well for you in life. What you must do is stop and listen before starting something. Always listen to the instructions first, patiently; that will save you from many situations. And one more detail, do not despise small beginnings. We start on our knees to get to know the area, we stand up when we are ready to go into battle. But it is on our knees that we strengthen and become wise. There is no rush, spend time learning, practicing and spend time praying and you will see how everything has a solution.

> "We start on our knees to get to know the area, we stand up when we are *ready* to go into battle."

At that moment I felt that my pastor was talking to me. I had a lump in my throat, and he seemed to know how broken I was in that place. You are people of great faith, right? I wanted to confirm we love the Lord; we are only his humble servants. Sandra answered wisely, and what are you doing here? I mean, what made you move from Venezuela to Aruba? Our plans were always to go to Miami, but it has taken a longer time than we expected and given the situations that are happening in Venezuela we wanted to come to Aruba in our waiting season. We have understood that when the wait can be long it is better to have a beach chair. - We laugh.

> "Is on our knees that we *strengthen* and become wise."

-I live in Miami, whoa! what a joy to know about your plans. What are you planning to do in Miami? - Whoa! another great coincidence if we can call it that - Luis said. - We should be moving next month if God allows it. We are waiting for some documents and voila, we are leaving. There, my brother has several paddle board businesses, so the plan is to help him and develop the business in other places. Our company is called "Walk on Water" and we do not only offer paddle board training, but also ecological tours. It is an excellent way to enjoy God's creation and meditate on the peace of His presence. Florida is undoubtedly one of the best places to paddle board. So, we want to go live there. - How awesome, I cannot wait to see you there. - You know, the versatility of a paddle board allows us to reach shallow water and narrow areas. It is also a sport that can be practiced by a child and an older person, a slim, stocky, or heavier person. We always make sure that all tours have a safety briefing, some basic land paddling instructions and our purpose is to add something else. We want to include the spiritual part. There are great learnings that we can take from this beautiful hobby, and each tour is approximately 2 hours and allows us to reflect on what we have learned. Tours are designed based on area, tide, and weather conditions. - Whoa! that is wonderful, I said that means that when I return to Florida, I already have a place to practice my new hobby.

We walked around the restaurants and the small shops, so colorful and cheerful. We enjoyed the beauty of that endearing place, knowing that we were there temporarily, but that the things that God was doing were for eternal purposes.

- Daughter, God's processes are perfect, nothing happens by chance, but with purpose. - Sandra assured me. Luis and Sandra had not come into my life by chance. They were a marriage full of love, like the one I had never known. They imparted so much wisdom to me and I needed to put them in writing. I told them a little about my life. - My father died when I was truly little, my mom and I moved

"Do not look for a new *beginning* in the heart, but in the Spirit. Fall in love with God."

to Miami, and in my adolescence, I got involved in a destructive relationship. I was 15 and at 18 I got pregnant and he left me for another woman. I quickly fell in love again and that one left me because he did not want to be the father of my daughter when he was so young.

I suffered a lot with that disillusion, so I decided to accept Jesus in my heart. But I think I wanted to help God and I met another man much older than me, and despite all the red flags and warnings, I married him. A month ago, I divorced after many mistreatments and threats. I told them that I had started blogging that afternoon and that I was ready for a new beginning.

They both looked at me in surprise at how young, I had lived so long. Sandra responded worried about what that new beginning could mean and said to me: - Daughter, be careful, do not look for a new beginning in the heart, but in the spirit. Fall in love with God. Your story is that of many young women who are lost without knowing their true value and make one mistake after another. This is the time to stop and know where you are going to put your heart. Put it on God, - she told me. She thinks I can be inspirational. Pamela being inspirational? Who would believe me? My life has not been an example for anyone until today. Could it be that God will change my destiny? Could there be a bigger and better plan? I think that all the mistakes of my life have been because I have thought that men are a life jacket ... the same one that perhaps if my father had used he would not have died at sea. But today I understood that there is something better than that. Who needs a life jacket when we have Jesus? Today I discovered that Jesus is my board of salvation. So, I titled the blog like this. I will give honor to the one who really makes me stand above all in the sea of adversities.

When the *wait* is long, it is better to be in a BEACH chair.

The *foolishness* of my youth

Reviewing our history leads us to look
through a magnifying glass and identify
where the errors were to correct them.

Eliazardo

*"Foolishness is bound up in the heart of a child;
The rod of discipline will remove it far from him."*

(PROVERBS 22:15, NASB)

Today I decided to get up early to go out to practice
paddle board with Luis and to be able to continue
writing on my blog in the afternoon. What a thrill! My
lifeline. Starting with this task is not an easy matter. It
means opening my heart to vulnerable areas of my
life. It means going back in time to tell my story a little
... And share what I learn, as I learn.

The idea makes complete sense with what my psychologist Lisa has told me what to do. Sometimes reviewing our history leads us to be able to look with a magnifying glass and identify where the errors were, to correct them. I am clear that the absence of a father during my upbringing, played a fundamental role in many of the mistakes I made. But I also recognize that my mom did an exceptional job trying to raise me as best she could. She was a stylist and I do not know how she managed, but she always made time for me. I spent long hours in the beauty salon helping her, I passed the broom, helped charge clients, sometimes simply entertained people when she was late.

But there was also time for me. We ate mostly outside because in the little time we had left in the afternoons it was not enough to prepare food and do my homework at school. We experienced a lot of financial shortages; I cannot deny it. We almost always shared the plate of food. We lived in a small apartment and we did not have great luxuries. We also did not go to church often, only on special occasions. But we did know of the existence of God; that was never questioned in my house. My mom decided to make me her most important assignment and put her own life aside to take care of mine. She never thought of remarrying. At least, if she did, did not tell me. But I think I would have liked to have a stepfather. Maybe that would have helped a little. I do not know.

The sound of the door surprises me and brings me out of my thoughts. I run to see who knocks and to my beautiful surprise it was Sandra.

-Hello Sandra, what are you doing here?

-I came to bring you breakfast, my girl. I know that you will be going with Luis to practice paddle board and you need to have strength.

Whoa! you should not have bothered, what a nice touch. Can you come in? Can you stay with me while I eat?

Sandra agreed and we started talking. Hey, girl, she asked intrigued. How was it that you became so young in a destructive relationship? Didn't your mother notice? Oh, Sandra, it was not her fault. I must admit that from a noticeably young age I was very amorous. There was always some boy I liked at school, there was always an illusion going through my mind. She was always trying to model a good example for me and guide me on that. But when I got to high school, I saw this tall boy with green eyes, a little long curly hair, he was blond and, in my eyes, he was perfect. He was not a student; He worked as part of a team of builders at the school. I tried awfully hard to make him notice me and after a while I did it. He started to look at me, he greeted me as I passed, and I felt like the luckiest woman in the world. Well, the luckiest girl in the world. I was barely 15 years old and I did not know what I was getting into. His name was Alberto.

We started spending time in the corners outside the school. My friends told me: "He is an old man for you", "Do not pay attention to him". I thought they were envious. I did not listen to anyone. Alberto was 22 years old, he was Cuban, and I confess that I lived enchanted with his accent, so manly in my eyes.

I continued talking. - We continued seeing each other and I did not hesitate to tell my mom. Anyway, I thought I was meeting the love of my life. My mom did not agree at all and strongly reprimanded me, even punished me. She began to make it exceedingly difficult for me to spend time with Alberto. Even my friends went against me; they did not understand our love. We kept insisting on seeing each other in secret and he was my best accomplice. One afternoon after leaving school I see Alberto in the distance beckoning me from a car. I approached with enthusiasm and he said to me: - Come with me, I just bought this car and I want us to have an ice cream.- It was the first time that we were going to be completely alone and out of the school area. My mom was not going to be able to stop me from spending time alone with him. My heart was beating fast.

We went for a ride in his car "for an ice cream" and continued walking around Miami. Suddenly we stopped at a small apartment in an area that I did not know. He invited me in, and I honestly did not want to, but I did not want to disappoint him either. I fearfully agreed without knowing that that day I would lose the most valuable thing that God gives to a woman, and in a forced way. I did not understand what had happened, but he wanted to justify it. I felt pain, shame, and fear.

I was sorry I had gotten myself into that situation and full of shame for what had happened. I had not thought for a second that would happen. It seemed like an unreal moment. A nightmare. It was my heart's desire to take care of my virginity until marriage, that was what my mom taught me, and I had cultivated that dream. Now I had forever disappointed her, God, and myself. He was indifferent, it seemed that for him it was completely normal. And he laughed at my "drama". He told me that he loved me and that was the natural thing that happened when two people loved each other. I felt that the world was falling apart. In the silence, from that dark room I cried out to God to help me. Immediately I could feel a heat that covered me from head to toe and covered my nakedness. Without knowing it, His presence and His mercy were with me. But I also knew that it was the beginning of something that God did not approve of.

The days passed without seeing each other again and the shame every day made me more anxious. I knew absolutely nothing about our future. I did not even know if I could be pregnant; he was completely ignorant of that subject. After a few weeks he returned to school and was a little distant with me. I did not understand his reaction and I innocently approached him to ask what was going on. He responded very seriously by asking me what time I was leaving so we could talk. I was extremely interested and worried, I responded and showed myself available to this "conversation". He was only looking for me with a truly clear intention: to continue that pattern that I did not know how to stop.

Confusion wrapped around me. I got used to it and began to think that this was love that love was like that; that I should feel grateful that he loved me so much that he endured my ignorance. If I asked him for explanations or refused, he threatened to leave me. - No, take it easy, girl, if you do not want to, it is okay with me, here we leave it, we're done, you go your way and I go mine. - That was his harsh response. For almost three years I agreed to this relationship that I called dating ... and he did not even call me. He was only looking for me on "the occasion". My mom knew that I was in communication with him, but she did not even imagine what I was up to. I had become an expert liar and was in a codependency relationship. The value that I gave myself was the one that he assigned me, that is, none. That was a "disgust-dating." One day at school I started feeling terribly upset, with a stomach ache. I came home throwing up and feeling that everything was spinning. My worried mom took me to the hospital. Her surprise was to discover that I was pregnant! I saw her turn pale in front of me and I did not even know what to say. I tried to explain as best I could what was going on and wanted to sell her the story that it was a stable relationship with a promising future. I explained that he had his own apartment, a vehicle, and that everything would be fine between us after high school.

The next day I went to school eager to see him and tell him what was going on. I really did not know what his reaction would be, but I never anticipated what I would discover. When I told Alberto about the pregnancy, he insulted me as if I had done something wrong. Tears ran down my cheeks but that was not the worst part. When his insults ended, their truths began.

Alberto had a girlfriend with whom he lived with and planned to get married. That person was not me. He had shamelessly played with me all this time. But according to him, it was my fault. He put all the responsibility on my shoulders for having "seduced" him. In the end, it was me who looked at him first, and he had simply responded as "what did you think would happen, I'm a man." So, I was playing with fire, and I finally got burnt, and I had to face it alone. He had another life in which I had no space, a life of which I had no knowledge at all. I never saw Alberto's face again.

Months passed, and my mom and I faced this situation together. My little girl was born in the summer and I was 18 years old. I did not know what I was going to do with my life, but I knew I had to be a mother. I decided to call her Penelope Sofia. Penelope because there was a popular song that seemed to describe me: the one that she sits waiting for his return. And Sofia because it was the name that resounded deep inside me, although I did not understand it. Then I found out that it meant wisdom. I wanted to think that it had all been a mistake, a lie, a bad joke, or a nightmare.

We lovingly call her PitaSofía. She brought joy, hope, and a pure love to my life. Within my lack of knowledge and youth, I managed to make a significant prayer: Lord, just as you adopted me as your daughter when my father abandoned me, so do now be the father of my daughter also. Do with her as you have done with me. I promise to be the best mom I can, I promise to imitate my mother's example, but please take the role of her Father, God. I cannot do this without you. Amen."

I felt that this simple prayer without great theology was released with sincere words and enormously powerful.

-And they were, daughter, they were," replied Sandra. Whoa, daughter, your story with that man is extraordinarily strong. Have you forgiven him?

- I wonders. I think so. We continued our conversation and her advice left me inspired to write on my blog my "take a way" of our beautiful talk.

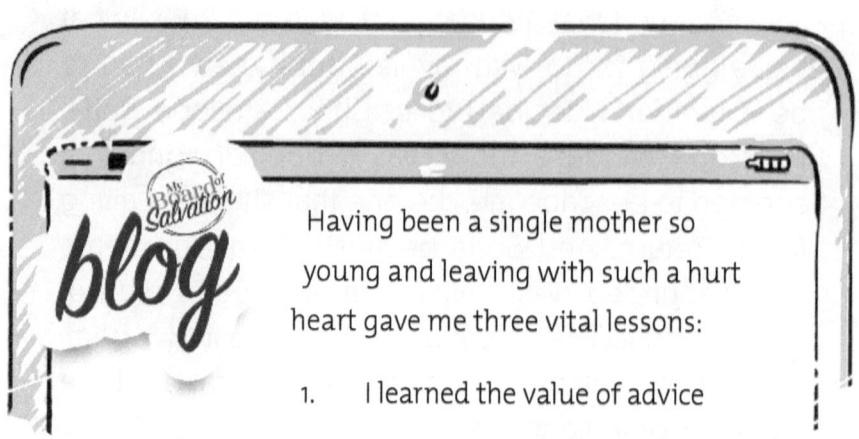

Having been a single mother so young and leaving with such a hurt heart gave me three vital lessons:

1.   I learned the value of advice

- There is wisdom in the multitude of councils.
- Many tried to stop me, and I went into a deep hole like a derailed train.

2. I discovered the value of obedience.
   - We do not need to understand why, just obey.
   - I was able to understand the Proverb that says: "Son, don't abandon your mother's teaching." Mothers certainly see what one cannot understand in their limited awareness of life.

3. I understood that you should not play with fire.
   - I sat in the saddle of the mockers and paid the price.
   - I used folly and they took advantage of my innocence.

But I also learned other things.
   - I learned to forgive.
      * When I look back, I can see that he was as guilty as me. I cannot feel like the victim of the situation because I was not. It is true that he took advantage of my innocence. It is true that he forced something that I did not want. It is true that he was a bad man.
      * But I decided to take responsibility for what I did, so that I can correct it and never

make the same mistake again. I admit that I looked at the physique and did not consider any of the signs that told me that he was not a suitable person for myself.

* I did not listen to the advice of my friends and my mother. In a dangerous situation, I lied, and did not respect the law of my own school by running away with him. I was reckless and took risks that were not controlled at all. I kept in a relationship that was not healthy at all and I did not tell anyone about the double life I was leading. I alone went into the lion's mouth hoping not to be devoured.

* Today I take responsibility for making a change.

* Today I also decide to forgive him. I forgive him because even recognizing all the things he did and how much damage he caused me, today I understand that he was a broken person with a past that marked him negatively, and that he has not known how to become a man to take responsibility for his life, leaving behind the lies and go for what really matters.

* Life always makes us pay the consequences of what we do wrong. Therefore, what happens to him in his future is not in my hands, but in the hands of God and his own acts.

* It is in my hands to forgive him so that I can let go of that glass that cuts my hand

and be able to continue a life of love for my daughter without letting the memory of who her father is tarnish the purity that my Penelope Sofía's eyes radiate.

* I decide to forgive him and not speak ill of him to my daughter and tarnish an image of someone she will never meet.

* I decide to introduce my daughter to the father who never abandons: God.

* I promise to tell her the whole truth from the moment she becomes aware of it and help her heal the wounds that both of us caused by being irresponsible.

* And finally, I forgive myself. I forgive myself for my ignorance, my foolishness, and my lack of judgment. I am released from all bondage that I established with that man in the name of Jesus. And from now on I decide to be free and happy to be the best mom I can be.

If this blog has touched your life, share it on your social networks under #Myboardofsalvation

Chapter

6

A surprise *falls*

In marriages there are natural waves of the couple itself, but there are other waves that are created by man and can be very dense.

Elisa Ilardo

"You rescue me from the violent man. Therefore, I will give thanks to You, O Lord, among the nations, and I will sing praises to Your name."

(2 SAMUEL 22.49-50)

I left my room around noon. I spent a few hours writing on my blog, which I love, and my plans for the day were delayed. Tomorrow I am going back to Miami and I must go paddle boarding at least once more.

I ran to the beach to look for Luis and I did not see him. I wandered from one place to another, but it was in vain; I could not see him. I went back to the hotel looking for Sandra to see if she knew of his destination.

- Oh yes, he goes to the marina many times at noon. There is a group of people who want to paddle board in a place without waves. Look it up and you will find him there. - I did not know where I was, but I followed her instructions and on such a small island it was not difficult to find.

-Luis - I spotted him in the distance on his board and started calling him.

- Hello, girl, how nice to see you, are you coming to practice today?

- Of course, I must get out of here like an expert. I'm going back home tomorrow.

-Then, come, leave the money with the guy in the cabin and get here, we will leave in a group. - Running, I paid and joined this adventure. I was sure that it would be easier than the day before. I put on my life jacket, and for this adventure, I had to get on the board from the pier, instead of entering through the water. It looked easy, but it was not. I did it on my knees, so I would not start my journey badly. Success, difficult yes, but possible. I had high expectations, I felt like an expert. I was super ready. There were always boats leaving towards the sea through the channel in which we were in.

- But Sandra said there was no waves - I said thinking aloud.

- No, baby, there is no natural waves, but the boats create them. It is like in marriages. There are

84

some that handle waves that are natural to the couple itself, but there are other waves that are man-made and can be very dense.

-We already started, Luis, we already started exceedingly early with the teachings ... - We laughed with my evident sarcasm.

I married Manuel full of expectations and dreams, as we all do. Just as I had entered that marina. Thinking I knew what I was doing. I idealized everything. I thought he was a charming prince, everything seemed to be perfect. We arrived home from the honeymoon; we were so happy. Manuel had to return to his businesses, which had been abandoned by my "demands." That is what he told me. I kept him busy helping me organize the details of the wedding, "how inconsiderate", and then he had to please my "tantrum" by leaving for a week of honeymoon. How could I be so inconsiderate? He had an important business; he was a construction architect. He had employees in charge, responsibilities to attend and here I am, with my childishness wanting to celebrate my first wedding. This was his third wedding, so he had experience and knew that we should not put so much effort into it. What were you thinking, Pamela?

"In *marriages* there are natural waves from the couple itself, but there are other waves that are created for our humanity and they can be very dense"

That morning we returned from the honeymoon and Manuel left everything lying in the new house, still empty, without furniture, and went back to work. I had packed suitcases, gifts, wedding decorations and the dresses of the celebration. I made a silly decision and left everything behind to visit my mother, to spend some time with her and my daughter. I went with them to fix my hair after the beach days, I did some shopping for dinner and I became distracted.

Upon returning to the house, what a tremendous surprise I had! The house was organized, at least it seemed so, but full of photographs taped to the walls. I approached to see what it was about, anticipating something beautiful ... I was curious and before my terrified eyes I saw a photograph of "my untidiness". Everything I had misplaced before I left had been photographed and placed as a gallery in our new home. I did not understand the concept.

My belongings were no longer where I had left them and thousands of thoughts flashed through my head, except the truth. I searched the whole house trying to find Manuel and our things. For my peace of mind, upon arrival in our room his things were properly placed on the bathroom vanity and his clothes folded next to the mattress that was still on the floor. Manuel was not there.

I went outside to look for him and it was then when I had my biggest surprise. All my belongings, including my wedding dress, were in the trash can. "If you are not able to take care of the house in which I placed you, if you cannot keep your things tidy, you do not leave me alternatives; you can't have them. I had to take care of my belongings, because obviously you do not know how to do it. I think I married a little girl; you have to grow up or you're going to lose me." These were his reprimanding words for my terrible action. And the nightmare had begun.

The thoughts and memories had filled my head in such a way that I forgot to pay attention, and suddenly ... this big boat came out and generated a wave so dense that it knocked me over. The problem was that between the wave and my proximity to one of the docks and my lack of coordination in swimming, I was under the pier and holding one of its columns.

-How scary, Luis, help me, look I did not come to die in Aruba!

-What? Die girl? Of laughter may be...! - Come on, give me your hand. Nothing happened. Luis helped me to get up and using my legs and all my strength I tried to get on the paddle board again. Four times I tried without success. And at the fifth I got on and as I stood, I fell again. "I have already fallen more times today than on my first day, how is this possible?"

"Concentrate, recognize where you are, calm down and focus on getting ahead." That was the same thing I thought that first night: I must pay more attention; I am a married woman and I must take better care of my husband to get this relationship off the ground.

As I paddleboarded among these boats, so many memories came. He had a 32-foot boat that he loved as much as his life. He explained to me that he managed his properties on a budget and that his biggest investment of money was in his boat, and that I could never compete, because his boat generated business for him. He said to me:

- Pamela, this marriage cannot cost me more than $2,000 a month. I assigned 5% of my monthly income to add you to my life. Any expense over $2,000 must be assumed by you. You must find that money to avoid breaking us.

-I was 5% of his life?

When Manuel and I met, we used to enjoy the same activities, we both loved the beach. What happened to us? He was always so gallant, chivalrous, gentle... But I remember that night he hit the walls and screamed, shook my shoulders with the desire to hit me, and was enraged at a level I never knew. Perhaps something he ate or drank caused that reaction. That was not Manuel. I had to concede to be intimate with him even though I did not want to, to try to calm him down. It was my fault. I should have noticed that my outfit that night was very provocative. My friends took a lot of my time at that party and I am sure that made him feel overwhelmed, perhaps unappreciated.

> "Recognize where you are, *calm down* and focus on getting ahead."

I should have been wiser. I must act as a Christian woman. How is it possible that I do not know how to behave? Those were my thoughts at that time. He was so willing to accompany me to my best friend's birthday party. He was the only male at the party. Sure, it was a friends-only party, but the other husbands do not care much about their wives and leave them alone. He will not let me go anywhere alone; he takes care of me.

Suddenly, boom!

-Pamela, are you okay? Luis asked. I was on my knees on the board and I did not even know how I got there. I hit a navy buoy head-on, one of those tall as a pole. At the time I did not know what hit the board and I fell to my knees. Frustrated, I sat down on my board and Luis approached me to ask if I was okay. He noticed me quite distracted; I was absent thinking about how the situations happened with Manuel.

-I do not know if I told you, Luis, but just a month ago I got divorced. He had a boat and being in this place has awakened many memories.

- I said honestly. "Easy, daughter, healing is a process," he commented, as he sat down on his board to accompany me.

- Can I ask why you got divorced?

-The correct question would be why did we get married?

- What do you mean, daughter? Is it that you knew before?

- Yes, Luis, I did know. Deep down I did know. There were so many unworked areas in my life, I was looking for a father and I was looking for an older man. I felt guilty for so many mistakes and accepted his mistreatment as part of my punishment. And why not say so? Economic factors also influenced me. I was seeking relief from my status as a single mother, and wanted a father for my daughter. It is shameful to admit it, but I went as a sheep to the slaughterhouse. I did not trust myself and did not trust God enough, so I had decided to help Him find me a husband.

-What made you decide to divorce? - He asked intrigued.

-I endured a lot. He would kick me out of the house or leave when he got mad. He gave me physical possessions and then humiliated me, yelled, and intimidated me. He yelled at my daughter and made us feel intimidated. He would show me his weapon and made me understand that I should never push him to use it. I never confronted him. I feared him. Manuel was a man 20 years older than me and very jealous. He was Mexican and had always lived in cultural maleness, he had suffered much abuse from his father and there was a lot of bitterness in him. I do not think he was a bad man, because he had particularly good times. But one day a pole in the water hit me and made me see.

-What do you mean? – He wonders.

- That a great surprise led me to fall on my knees in the presence of the truth. I discovered that Manuel visited places of prostitution constantly. He had a very dark sexual life to which he wanted to take me if I stayed, and for my daughter I decided to escape. When I found out he got upset, indirectly threatened to kill me, if I destroyed his reputation. I saw the worst in him. He shouted at me: "You are crazy, you have the perfect man and you want to leave him." He was sure to be a victim of my dis-love. It was a long process of separation before he filed for divorce. That is when I really learned how to pray. He was constantly unfaithful, and he abused me verbally, sexually, and psychologically. I spoke to my Pastor and they warned me: "If you don't get out of there, that man is going to kill you. His jealousy, his character and his conduct, in general, make him a strong candidate to do more." I prayed, fasted for days. One day he confessed to me that if he did not leave, he could end up killing me. God took care of me, Luis. God saved me. I did what God told me, fasting and prayer, and this happened:

"So humble yourselves before God. Resist the devil, and he will flee from you. Come close to God, and God will come close to you. Wash your hands, you sinners; purify your hearts, for your loyalty is divided between God and the world. Let there be tears for what you have done. Let there be sorrow and deep grief. Let there be sadness instead of laughter, and gloom instead of joy. Humble yourselves before the Lord, and he will lift you up in honor." (James 4:7-10)

blog

Recognizing that you are in an abusive relationship is difficult, especially when that man sends you combined signals. He treats you like a queen, but he also mistreats you. He believes himself superior to others and isolates you. He can give you many things, but he wants to be the center of attention in your life, for good and for bad. These men are charming at first, but they are manipulative. They lack empathy and are envious by nature. They do not like taking orders and are never vulnerable. When you meet a man of the narcissistic type, it is very possible that he will become an abuser.

I will share with you below, the vision that God gave me about my relationship with this man. It is called "Beauty and the Beast", but it has nothing to do with the original version of the movie:

I was walking hand in hand with this strong, manly, rough-looking man, who some time ago was very handsome, but whose bitterness and years have hidden his natural attractiveness. I looked pretty, happy, simple, radiant, but casual. The beast turns surprisingly as I sing a nice song and vomits on me. From my hair to my feet, everything was stained with his vomit. I open my eyes in surprise and look at him for an answer. He acts surprised and gently apologizes to me and says he could not help it. He asks me not to worry, that he loves me anyway; that he will guide me because I don't see clearly; that he will defend me from the people who criticize me; that he will take me away from those who look at me now strange; and that I will never be alone.

He does not clean me, but the rain and the wind are removing the residue of so much garbage. Time passes and when I have forgotten the first violation and once again, I start dancing while I walk among the gardens, he turns once more and vomits on me. I am no longer surprised, now I cry. He hugs me and says, "See how I love you despite your trash?" I am confused. I begin to stop understanding who the trash belongs to. I start to feel like the trash is me. After this happens several more times, my gaze turns gray and my head does not get up to greet the day. I hold on tight to his arm hoping that his mercy will never leave me.

Seeing this vision of myself and who I had become, I understood that I was in a relationship of emotional, psychological, verbal and sometimes even sexual abuse. He has never hit me physically, but he had given my soul the most monstrous blows, leaving fear and intimidation, insecurity, and confusion. I knew I could not get out of there alone. I needed a support network. I needed help.

My precious sister, if this is you or you know you have a friend in this situation, act. Share this blog and tag #Myboardofsalvation to know that you saw it. Together we can find a way out. Send an email to mitabladesalvacion@gmail.com and we will help you find a way out. You are not alone. Enough of the abuse of women.

 SHARE

God makes
my HEART
smile.

7

Waters of death and waters of life

"But those who drink the water I give will never be thirsty again. It becomes a fresh, bubbling spring within them, giving them eternal life."

(JOHN 4:14)

It is the day to return to normality. My daughter and my mother, Naomi, are waiting for me at home and I must go back to work. I wanted to study fashion design because it is something, I have been passionate about since I was a child. But how difficult is it! My employment is in a store in Brickell for a Brazilian designer. I work with the owner every day, but what a temper! What character does that woman have! But no way, it is part of my learning process. Someday I will have my own clothing line and I think I will also call it My Board of Salvation! How about making decent clothes to go paddle boarding on the beach? I want to be comfortable and not show too much skin that has cost me so many tasty desserts.

I must go see Sandra and Luis before I go, and exchange phone numbers. I want to see them once they move to Miami. We cannot lose communication.

-Hi Sandra, how are you? I came to see you and say goodbye - I happily greeted my new spiritual mother, Sandra.

-Daughter, are you leaving today? - she asked amazed

-Yes, I only came for 3 days, responsibility calls me. But I want to see you again. When are you moving to Miami?

- Soon, daughter, soon. Give me your number and we will dial you once we know the date, to go meet your daughter and your beautiful mom.

We held each other tight as if we had known each other for years, both knowing that we were going to miss each other.

I walked to the beach to say goodbye to Luis before I left. Riding on that plane without saying goodbye would be terrible. I love goodbyes. Perhaps because I did not have the opportunity to say goodbye to my Daddy, as I said.

I spotted Luis in the distance and called his name. I ran to him as if we were old friends that I had not seen in a long time.

-Luis, Luisito, I am going to miss you - I shouted excitedly.

-Oh, my girl, you are leaving, but how could we love you so much in just two days? - we laugh.

It had been a short time, but so emotional. I learned so much with them!

It was early in the morning and I noticed that there was a group waiting for him. But they were all in white and there were no tables. I asked:

- Luis, what are you doing, is there a wedding on the beach?

- No, my daughter, although good, the wedding of the lamb. But no, they are baptisms. Are you baptized? I advanced to answer.

–Yes, I did that once, they told me it was my turn. He looked at me strangely and started to tell me what it was about.

-Daughter, baptism is the moment when you decide to die to be reborn in Christ. It is when, after having accepted the sacrifice of Christ on the cross, you decide to completely abandon the old creature and die to sin. You submerge yourself in the water as an act of submission and representing the burial of your flesh. When you rise out of the water you are a new creature in Christ. In Galatians it says that all who have been baptized into Christ have clothed themselves with Christ. Jesus said and is documented in John 3:5): "I assure you; no one can enter the Kingdom of God without being born of water and the Spirit."

- Whoa! Luis, if I was baptized already, isn't it true that I cannot do it again? - I asked.

- Daughter, if you were aware of the step you were taking, it is not necessary. But if today you have understood what this symbolic moment is about and you want to enter the water and die to self to live in Him, let it not be me who stops you, - he answered me.

After he said this, he continued baptizing. I sat on the sand to enjoy that beautiful moment. I looked at them with jealousy. Seeing them come out of the water with so much joy was wonderful. There was a great difference, which I did not experience when I was baptized 5 or 6 years ago following instructions. I do not even remember the day.

My heart was pounding, I felt it would give me a heart attack, and I said to God in my mind: "If this is something I have to do, tell me something very specific to convince me." At that time, Luis said to those who were observing and had not yet decided:

-If you are asking God for a specific test to convince you, understand that He forces no one. When he said those words, I jumped off the sand and ran into the water in tears to be baptized. I knew he had answered me audibly through him and would not let this warning pass without acting.

When my head was submerged in the water, hundreds of brief memories passed through my head. It was like a review of my life passed before my eyes. They lifted me out of the water, and I felt that something was submerged in the water. A part of me was trapped in the water and I was free. I was jumping with happiness and laughing while crying. Ineffable joy touched me inside and manifested itself.

I hugged everyone without stopping jumping. I was energetic at a level never known to me.

-You have made the most important decision of your life. Do not look back. - Luis told me.

-See you, Luis, see you when you get home. I love them! Thank you, I love you so much, I am leaving happy!

- I said goodbye screaming while walking. I was late for the airport, but this was a divine appointment that God had planned for me.

I managed to catch the plane, but I was literally the last to board. From that seat I managed to look at the beautiful beaches. I confess that seeing the sea always confronted me. I grew up thinking that if I looked a lot to the sea, if I search it long enough, maybe I would find my father floating somewhere on some beach. On some island, on a raft. I was so small when he left us. My dad was the most beautiful love of my life, until today I miss him.

I remember his smile as if I had seen him yesterday. I remember when he held me on his legs in the garden of the house. I remember running to the door screaming: "Daddy, Daddy" ... I felt that the moment he arrived from work, got out of his Jeep, and entered our house on that hill in Rincon, seemed eternal. My dad was a man with a very white complexion, tall, blond, with beautiful green eyes. An American from Boston who had decided to make Puerto Rico his home. He fell in love with the waves of Rincón and the heat of its people. My mom met him when she was just 18 years old and according to the story he used to tell, he had never seen a more beautiful brunette than Naomi. My mom was shy, a little quiet and of a simple character. It is extremely easy to make her laugh. She is not witty like my dad was. I inherited character and eyes from him. But my mom is an easy woman to be loved. Helpful, consistent, stable, responsive. A faithful follower of any plan that seems right to her. She is the best grandmother my daughter could have.

My dad and mom got married noticeably young. My mom was 20 and my dad was 23. My dad was always at sea. He used to surf, dive and fish. And that was his profession. He was a professional fisherman and worked for the tuna fleet out of Mayagüez, Puerto Rico. A horrible November 15 he left at three in the morning for his work as he used to do every day, and never returned. The sea swallowed him up. His body was never found.

- You are too small to understand - that is what everyone told me. I was barely five years old, but I was so aware, I remember everything. I remember the search, the expectation, I remember the pain, I remember the absence. His departure left deep consequences in my being.

Knowing that one day I will see him again is not enough; it is not a relevant consolation to me. I would have liked to keep him present at every birthday, at every sharing on the beach, in every important decision. I would have liked him to teach me so many things, to introduce him to my friends, I would have been such a proud daughter. Being an only child, loneliness feels even greater; you become the consolation of your mother, her best friend, her sister. Only 21 years of age difference between her and me made it easy for us to become so close. But having the character of my dad made me sometimes be the strong figure of the house.

I remember when my mom asked me about moving to the United States. I was 7 years old. I did not even know that there was more to the world than Rincon, my corner. But she showed me photos and I found it interesting to visit other beaches. Maybe my dad was there. He anticipated that I would have to learn a new language, Dad's language. The language she did not speak. I never anticipated how difficult the change would be. But we went on a new adventure to escape a painful reality. Today, 21 years later, I am going back to the place that became our home: Miami.

Chapter

8

Wisdom cries: the "leash" that I cannot lose

"Joyful is the person who finds wisdom, the one who gains understanding. For wisdom is more profitable than silver, and her wages are better than gold. Wisdom is more precious than rubies; nothing you desire can compare with her."

(PROVERBS 3:13-15)

- PitaSofia, mami* arrived. That is how I exclaimed when I got to my house in Miami. I clearly remember that the day before I knew I was pregnant I felt physically ill. I felt weird. I struggled a lot with thoughts of suicide, so I thought maybe it was my time to die and I was ok with it. So, I prayed that night and said to the Lord, "I am not asking you to give me health, give me what I need."

**. Mommy

I thought that what I needed was to die, and He decided to give me life through my daughter and give me the wisdom that I did not have. Because that daughter of mine is a gallon of wisdom. The next day I found out that I was pregnant. I remember that a great pain took over my heart because inside me I knew that Alberto was not a person with whom I should be. I wanted it to be the love of my life, but inside me I knew that would not happen.

It has been 10 years of that, and I still see her as that little baby.

-Mommy, it is good that you arrived well, how do you feel? - asked my daughter.

-Penelope Sofía, I am your mother, not your daughter. - I must constantly remind her of her age; she is too mature for her age. She is just 10 years old and has already started middle school because they have skipped grades. But she is going to become my older sister the way she is going, I thought while caressing her beautiful hair.

-I bought you some things, my love - I said affectionately.

-Oh, mommy, you should not have bothered. This trip was for you and not to bring me gifts. Also, I am not missing anything.

- She never ceases to amaze me with her answers. I cannot anticipate what she will answer me. Who is inside this little girl?

I remember that the day I had the pregnancy test something very strange arose within me. There was sadness and great fear, but at the same time there was the hope of great joy. There was a sense of relief as anticipating that the little person who was coming was going to help some way. I did not know how, but that is how I felt it and from that day on I knew that her name was Penelope Sofia. I kept that a secret inside me because my mom was furious with me and I was afraid to speak to her. But months later in the pregnancy I mentioned the name to her, she searched the Internet for its meaning and with sincere sarcasm she told me: "Daughter, Penelope Sofia means what you need."

- What? I asked innocently.

-Patience and wisdom. - My mother answered.

At that moment, I remembered that little prayer that I said the day before I knew I was pregnant, when I asked God to give me what I needed, and the Lord gave me Penelope Sofia.

- Mom, do you want me to bring you a tea or something to eat? Grandmother is at work, but I have already done my homework and I can attend to you.

-No, my baby, I want you to let yourself be loved. I want to watch TV with you, tell me what you have done, and what you would like to do. Would you like to go with me to buy a paddle board? - I asked her.

- Mom, paddle board? Do you know how to do that? She asked in surprise.

- Yes, daughter, I learned this weekend in Aruba.

-So, let us go. I also want a paddle board, but, can you explain to me how you did it without knowing how to swim?

How can that small piece of flesh be so full of intelligence and wisdom? She is a living portrait of her grandfather: intelligent, with character, protective, those green eyes, her stature, her face ... She has dark hair like mommy, but otherwise it is a portrait of "Daddy". PitaSofía smiles and two small dimples appear in those rich little cheeks that reveal that she still a little girl.

-Well, daughter, go change and we will go.

-I said. As I waited for her, I contemplated her toys, dolls, her pink bicycle that she no longer uses. Time has passed so quickly. She grows at unthinkable speeds and will soon take flight. These years have passed so quickly. Could it be that I have missed seeing her grow up?

We went to a nearby shopping center and along the way I tried to find out how my daughter's life was going. Her answers were short, but I was interested to know how her days were. We entered a gigantic store that from the outside you can see paddle boards. I asked her, intrigued:

- Daughter, would you really like me to buy you one? It could be our new hobby together ...

- Well, mom, it sounds good, but let us see the prices, I do not think they are cheap. - She answered a little worried. -

Oh, calm down, girl, "I got this" - I answered very sure, without having the slightest idea of what I was saying.

- Hello, I am looking at the paddle boards, can you help me? - I asked an employee.

- Of course, what are you looking for? "All around", "cruisers", "for race" or for "surfing with paddle"? - The employee replied, revealing my ignorance.

- Well, I am starting, I would like a wide one so as not to fall. - I replied, hoping he would show a little mercy to this newbie who was trying to impress her 10-year-old daughter.

- In that case I recommend one of these. They are big, a little heavy, but it will give you a lot of stability. And today they are on sale. There is a 25% discount so if you take it today, it will only cost you $1,250 dollars.

- What? - My eyes widened as much as my mouth. He smiled like someone who is used to pulling down newbies like me from the clouds.

- Yes, it is a little difficult to get a better price on a board like this. But I have cheaper ones - and he took me over to another area confident that he was giving me the super deal.

- These start at $799 and while smaller, they are at a tremendous price to start. At this point the shame ran out of my pores. This boy does not know that I live with my mom and daughter because there is no way I can pay for an apartment alone; that my car was a gift and that I don't have half of what he is asking for.

- Okay, thanks, do not bother, I will have to wait a bit to buy one. - I answered as sophisticated as I could and started walking with my daughter holding hands so that she would not ask any more questions. We both started laughing. It was not the first time that we went to a store and left terrified when seeing the prices.

-Well, then you went to the beach - my daughter interrupted the embarrassing moment to make me feel distracted. Always taking care of me, what a girl of mine!

- Yes, my little girl, I went to the beach and had a great time in Aruba. And you, what did you do these days? Completely ignoring my question, she answered with more intriguing questions.

- Did you meet new people? Something to tell. - She insisted.

- Yes, my love, I met genuinely nice people, but I will tell you later, tell me about yourself. - I replied.

- Mommy, you went to the beach for three days alone, you say you met new people, I want to know more ... - at this point I already sounded too interested.

-Hey, girl, but I am asking about you and you insist on returning the questions. What do you want to know? What happened? - I replied already a little upset.

Penelope Sofia is not one to give up too soon, but this time she was too incisive to know. I know that the subject of the sea is always a matter of care for her. A few seconds of silence after my confrontation and she raised her face with tears in her eyes.

- Oh, my girl, forgive me, I have not seen you in days and I was a burden, forgive me.

- I have taught my daughter that adults make mistakes too and we must be vulnerable. I believe in apologizing when I hurt her and when I am wrong, but this time, that was not the case.

"Mommy," she replied with a disapproving look that I had not seen before.

- I do not want you to fall in love anymore.

- We were at the exit of the store that faces the shopping center and her words sounded like a loudspeaker to my surprised ears. As soon as she finished saying the painful words that seemed to have cut her inside when she let them out, just as they cut me in the soul when listening to them, she faded in tears over me. I walked hugging her to a nearby sidewalk. I felt the warmth of her little body on me, her tears wet my shirt and it broke my heart with each one.

What is inside her guarded heart that I am about to discover?

- Daughter, don't you want mom to be happy? - I asked the dumbest question of my life. The words had come out of my mouth without knowing the damage they would cause.

- Can't you be happy if there is no man in your life? Are you not happy with Grandma and me? You do not love me, mommy, is that it, you do not love me?

- Her voice had risen like never, her face was red, her tears were real, her pain was deep. I have never seen my little girl cry and claim this way.

- Sorry, sorry, sorry, my girl ... Forgive Mom, of course I love you, I am happy with you and with Grandma.

- I did not know what to say ... I felt so ashamed. We sat on that bench in silence for minutes that seemed eternal. She cried in my arms, and I just hugged her and caressed her tender hair while thinking ... "How much damage I have done to my daughter. In ten years, I have not stopped looking for the love of a couple and have hurt her without wanting to."

-I want you to speak to me, Penelope Sofia, I want to know what you feel, what you fear, what worries you ...

- Mommy, I see my friends and it hurts.

-What hurts you, my girl? Seeing that they have a dad at home?

-Well, yes before, that hurt before. I saw my friends with their daddies, and I was jealous. But I became so attached to José, mommy, I love him so much. I wanted him to be my real dad, I do not know why he left. It was my fault?

-No, daughter ... - and she interrupted me suddenly to continue ...

-And then Manuel came, and even though he was so loud and sometimes bad with me, I thought he was going to stay. And he left. I do not want anyone else to come anymore. Mommy, I see you talking to men, how they look at you, I see you flirt, I am ashamed. I am ashamed to have so many "dads". Mom, at the end, everyone will leave. My dad does not even know me. I do not even know how it is to have one. I want it to be just the three of us. It does not even hurt to not have a dad anymore. What hurts me is that I feel like I do not have a mom either.

-Again, she melted into tears and each tear was a stab in my heart. What have I been doing? She is ashamed? How have I marked my daughter in this way? What deep pain in my heart! I felt faint at the sound of her words. How right! I remained silent and only managed to say: "Sorry."

We hugged out of that mall. Silent. It was the feeling of defeat that had affected me most in my life. I failed as a mom. I abandoned my daughter in life. I never envisioned myself in this situation. I thought I was looking for a home for you. In that search I did not realize that I destroyed the one I had with her.

- Daughter, today you have given your mother the most important lesson of her life. From this moment on, my most important role will be being a mom. I have been distracted by the life I wanted to have, and I have not known how to value the one I have. But I promise you something: that will change. I am young, yes, maybe not as mature as you ... - we laugh together. - But I can learn to be a mom as fast as I learned to paddle board. - I said smiling ...

> "A wise woman builds her home, but a foolish woman tears it down with her own hands."
>
> (Proverbs 14:1)

-Well, in that case, I must go and evaluate - we laughed out loud. I think the example of the board still does not give you much confidence.

- Mom, I know how to paddle board.

- Really? How so?

- My friend Natalia goes with her parents every so often. You met them on the birthday of Brazilian Jonathan.

- Well, being like that, let us make a group and we all go - I said.

- The important thing, mommy, is that you never take off the "leash", I do not know if they explained it to you. But as confident as you feel, that is what keeps you connected. Because of the leash you can save a life. - She said very confidently.

-Wisdom is with those who hear advice, that is what Proverbs 13:10 says, mom. Oh, and one other thing: now, please, do not fall in love again.

The "leash" keeps you connected to the board, just as prayer keeps you connected to God. - His voice, again. I need you God.

What a heavy night, I have a lot to think about ...!

9

He led me to *shore*

*"You intended to harm me, but God intended
it all for good. He brought me to this position
so I could save the lives of many peoples."*

(GENESIS 50:20)

It has been a week since I got home from my vacation
and I feel sad. What happened to the spirit with
which I arrived? I could not stop thinking about the
conversation with my daughter. What a great surprise
this girl has given me! How much did Joseph mean
to her! He was the first man she met in our lives. She
was just two years old when he appeared. I confess
that I had met several, it is a reality that staying alone
has been a challenge for me, but I never thought
it affected her. I was 20 years old, I really wanted
to give my daughter a responsible father. José
was handsome, tall and a gentleman. He had this
beautiful Colombian accent that melts me. It seemed

perfect. He only needed the horse to be a prince. He approached me at a social event and my eyes lit up with excitement. Beautiful green eyes looking at me ... I thought. I did not hesitate. I said inside: "I just met the love of my life." Without knowing him well, I already wanted to spend the rest of my life with that handsome young man.

We began to share, to spend time together and each moment at his side seemed like a dream. He was sweet, gentle, chivalrous, with a very docile temperament and always smiling. And to top it all off, he seemed to love my daughter. From the first time they saw each other, there was a connection between them. She even looked like him. "I hit the lottery," I said. I must admit that it was a blessing to have met him, because the pain of what happened later was what brought me to the feet of Christ. But it was a terrible pain to lose him. A pain like perhaps no other. Melancholy is knocking on my door and I do not want to let her in. My boss has given me the day off and I will take advantage of it. I will look for a place to practice paddle board.

I am going to know this beautiful river where a small group that I discovered online will go out to practice paddle board and they will have boards for rent. We were 4 people and two of them were experts. There was no wind or great challenges. It was truly a walk on water. A perfect day. But a memory from the past kept coming to my mind as if trying to torture me. Joseph. How could I not see it coming? My mom approved it from day one. My daughter loved him since she saw him enter. We all thought he was the right one. José's love for Penelope Sofía made me imagine that we would have the happiest family in the world. Every night he visited us, and we sang together, we put her to bed together, we went out to the parks together. We became a family in just 6 months of relationship. But one night, that night ... He came to visit us with a somewhat different face. My mom had taken Penelope Sofia for a walk to the mall. José looked worried.

-We need to talk. - he said. - I want us to talk about our relationship and our future. I did not hesitate, I said to myself: "He is nervous because he is going to ask me to marry him!" I felt butterflies fluttering in my stomach like never. I felt so lucky. I have never met such a special, sweet, and loving person with my daughter. We never had a fight, everything was wonderful between us, so I could not wait to hear it.

- Pamela, you came into my life to fill it with joy and color, you and Penelope Sofia fill me with joy, I have never felt so loved and so well received as I feel every time I visit you. I want you to know that I love you very much and that I love your daughter with all my heart. I see her as a daughter of my own and feel so proud when I hold her hand in the park; I think she even looks like me.

- As he spoke, my heart was pounding, my hands were sweating, and my tears came out without being able to avoid it. I just imagined our wedding day. I dreamed of that moment and was sure that he had a ring in his pocket to ask me to marry him. That was the long-awaited day. So, he went on to say:

-Honey, for this reason, I do not want to continue dating you without defining our relationship. It is important to me that you know that I have always wanted to marry in a church and have a traditional marriage as God demands. Although I do not currently attend any church, I would like to go to mass on Sundays as a family and make it a tradition. But for that very reason, I have a dilemma. I want you to excuse me because in these 6 months dating, I have never introduced you to my family and I want you to know the reasons why.

-I could not come to my house and tell my family that I am dating a single mother; they would not accept it. My family is very traditional, and we have never had someone with a child out of wedlock. And we want to keep it that way. For this reason, Pamela, we can continue to go out and have the relationship as it is now, but I do not want you to have expectations that we will have a future together, because that is not what is within the plan that I have for my life. .

-End of his speech and end of my heart. Literally, Pamela died. Trying to describe the brokenness I felt is impossible with words. The butterflies in my stomach turned into scorpions that were eating me from the inside out. I felt faint. I was not prepared for those words. It never crossed my mind to hear them. I gasped for breath, I felt like I was choking. The crying was so deep that I felt ashamed, I felt like a naked girl at school. If I plucked the hair from my head, it would not hurt as much. I could not pronounce words. We were both silent; only crying spoke. He comforted me with his hand, but with his words he had destroyed me. He did not go away, he cried with me, motionless.

Remembering that dark night weakened me terribly. I asked the coach to stop for a few minutes. We were close to the shore, so some took the opportunity to do tricks in the water. I just sat on the board. My legs in the water lowered the heat I was feeling inside me. With my eyes closed on my board, I remembered that great pain. That night I felt a bombardment of thoughts hitting my head like missiles. I was tormented. I listened to insults and offenses without stopping: "Darling, what did you think?"

"With the hand of God, *you will reach* the shore without noticing it, and you will do it rested."

-"Worldly and dirty woman"

- "You are not worthy of him; you do not deserve so much"

- "You are worth nothing and nobody will love you"

- "Your past will haunt you; you are a woman's crap and you don't deserve to be related to decent people"

- "You deserve to be beaten, spit on and abandoned." At that time, the enemy had sent an army of spiritual bullies to shout insults at me. From that moment on, my own image was broken along with my heart. Today on this board I look back and feel compassion. I remained with my eyes closed and had not noticed that my board had been moving. My feet reached out to touch the sand and I was startled by the touch. My board approached the shore without wanting to. It was as passive, as subtle, as Jesus when he came into my life. From the hand of God, you will reach the shore without noticing it, and you will do it feeling rested.

My heart was destroyed. I did not know how to get over that. I wanted to die. My mom invited me to a church that she had been visiting. Upon arrival, a sweet lady approached me and said: "You are a woman of courage who deserves to have hope. A virtuous, desired, and worthy woman. You deserve to be treated more like fragile glass; you are more valuable than precious stones. Your past does not define you. Jesus paid the price for your sin. You were created to be a co-heir, a suitable help, a crown of honor for your husband. Strength and honor are your clothing. Women like you can laugh at the days to come. They call you blessed." I must confess that I did not believe any of her words. Her name was Lisa. She was an associate pastor of the church and a

> "The will of God will always lead you to a *safe place*. To a place where you can stand firm."

professional psychologist. But she did not know me, and we did not know at that time that in addition to being my counselor, she would be one of my greatest friends. She saw me that day for the first time upon arriving at church and said that God spoke to her and gave those words to tell me.

-"It is the poem to the virtuous woman, Proverbs 31. That is, you, receive it," she said. Each of the words she spoke were the opposite of how I felt.

-That is not me, madam, you were wrong, or God was wrong - I answered with deep sadness.

It has been a long road. But that was how God brought me to shore. God's will, will always take you to a safe place. To a place where you can step on solid ground.

That dark night I felt that I had heard the final judgment on my life and with tears in my eyes and pain in my soul, I accepted the judgment and the penalty. I stayed in that relationship proposed by him. No future, no titles, but with its "advantages". Those were harmful months to my self-esteem. The damage to my self-esteem was so great that I was beginning to feel like a prostitute. I walked next to him feeling ashamed to accompany him. He was doing me a favor by letting me walk beside him. There were no limits to our relationship, and I gave myself completely as a woman. I thought

"In the mist of brokenness, our *hearts* become sensitive and we give space to God."

121

he was going to fall in love with me in such a way that he was going to forget all that conversation, ask for forgiveness and take me to the altar. It would give me the place I longed to have, although I thought I did not deserve it. But that never happened. I kept trying to seduce him to change his mind and I was unsuccessful in my attempts. One night we went to dinner together and we met some friends of his. That was going to be a sample to me of if my efforts were paying off. How would he introduce me? I was wondering.

- What are you doing here? - He asked his friends. The situation was uncomfortable, and he extended the greeting avoiding having to make the official presentation, until it was evident, and they asked about me. His response was almost as funny as it was embarrassing.

- Well, this is Pamela ... Eh ..., a companion, yes, my friend, I mean friend, like my best friend. - He said stammering.

I almost dare to add sarcastically, - like a sister. But doing so would burst the bubble of accumulated pain I was trying to control, and I did not want to cry in front of everyone. His friends realized the strange situation, but nothing was important anymore. That moment only finished annihilating my vain illusions. That same night I decided to try to save what I had left. If there was any dignity left, I had to leave, and I ended the relationship. I could no longer resist such humiliation. I was so hurt that my love became a great pain. I wished my resolution and determination would cause him to seek me out intently until I could forgive him. But it was in vain. That did not happen.

Despite the pain, I must admit that during the breakdown when our hearts become sensitive, we give space to God. There was no way to do it if I did not hold onto the Lord. That first day in church everyone realized how broken I was, but they did not know why. Just like Lisa, everyone showed me their love. So, I began to go every Sunday to church, as a place of refuge. I constantly cried out to the Lord to fix that relationship, to give him to me as a husband. I even tried to manipulate Him with Penelope to touch his heart. But it did not happen. I even went so far as to tell God that if He fixed my situation with José then I would give Him my life. If He did not fix it, I was only going to visit the church, but I was not going to give my heart to Him.

- If you give me what I want, I will give you what you want. - that was my "negotiation" with God. How incorrect and ignorant was my prayer. But God brought me to shore. He brought me closer to his heart and now I must heal my daughter, who was the victim of the situation.

blog *My Board of Salvation*

Sometimes we do not know where life takes us, where God wants to take us. We think things are going to be a certain way and you get a big surprise.

It makes me think ... When Joseph (the one from the Bible) was thrown into the cistern, he did not think he would survive that. Surely, he thought it would be the end. His life, even though he survived, was not easy after that experience. And in each of those tests it could be the end. But God took him to a safe place. He placed him in a hierarchical position and was a blessing to his brothers, the same ones who one day wanted to kill him.

Living a partner's contempt can leave you in a pit of despair. You do not know where you are going, and you question your real value. But God does not rate you based on your past, your social status, or your relationships. I discovered that He loves me. That if I am lost and I cry to Him, He will answer me; that in dangerous situations He will always take me to a safe place. That He loves me for who He is and not for who I am. That with Him I can walk confidently because He has promised to love me to the end of the world and if He says so, He will do it. If today you are standing in the middle of life, close your eyes, let go of everything and trust Christ, who will take your board to the shore and give you rest. You do not have to be perfect to be his girlfriend. If you are not ashamed of Him before men, He will not be ashamed of you before His Father.

If this message touches your life, share it on your social networks under #Myboardofsalvation - Can you give me a Like?

If you follow my *voice,* you will ARRIVE at a *safe* DESTINY.

10

A used
paddleboard

*"But he was pierced for our rebellion, crushed for
our sins. He was beaten so we could be whole.
He was whipped so we could be healed."*

(ISAIAH 5:5)

I have a joy in my heart that I cannot contain. Today,
Sandra and Luis come to live in Miami. They promised
to come to my house as soon as they arrived, and
my mother has prepared a delicious dinner for them.
My mother's heart is wonderful. This month after I
arrived from Aruba I recognized the beautiful value
of my family. I have enjoyed my daughter so much
in what she has called "Little Night Talks". I have also
been able to see the great woman I have in my mom.
We came to this country when I was just 7 years old
and she was a young widow of 28 years old, exactly
my current age. I remember that cold wind that

blew on my face when leaving the airport. It was a cold Christmas. From that moment I began to miss my country. Everything seemed giant and strange. I came from a small coastal town where everyone knew each other. But at just 7 years old I knew very well that my job was to take care of my mom. Daddy was always in charge but asked me to take care of her and watching over her when he was gone. That remained for me a permanent commission. Now I see that my daughter seems to do the same for me.

I always tried to make my mom feel safe and protected. My mom did not speak English; I spoke a little because I had learned from my dad. So, at a young age I started to be her translator, a job that I still have to this day. She had studied hairdressing when we lived in Puerto Rico, but she worked from home until we got here. When we arrived in Miami, we were staying with a distant relative of my dad. We slept in the same bed, so every night we practiced the questions and answers to go out the next day to find a job. It was like a game. Every night I played at owning a beauty salon interested in hiring my mom. I accompanied her to her appointments in case she needed a translation, but also because she had no one to leave me with. It was the coldest Christmas I can remember. I think I have visited more than 30 beauty salons that seemed like hundreds at my young age. My presence seemed to bother them a little. Some sarcastically asked her if the job was for her or me. Others recommended that she ask for a job in a childcare center; others did not even pay attention to her. I was both ashamed and sad for her, but I must admit I hoped that because it was going so badly, we would return to Puerto Rico.

Walking down Eighth Street we stopped for lunch and continued our appointments. But in that place, we met this strange man. He was male yet acted like a lady. My mom told me not to look at him. That was impossible. He looked at me making silly faces, causing me to laugh. He was the friendliest character I had known since my days there. It was very tempting to hear his stories; He spoke with a jovial accent pleasing to my ears. He was from Dominican Republic, and they called him Coco, he was the party of that place.

> "If you judge people without knowing them, you could limit the *blessings* God has for your life."

My mom was reluctant to talk to him because she had been raised in a very traditional Catholic environment and my grandfather forbade her to be approached by anyone with a description like that. But Coco won my heart. I wanted to listen to him all afternoon. He approached us, started the conversation, and wanted to meet us. I made the task easy for him, my mom not so much.

- My mom is the best hairdresser in the world - I said. - We are looking for a job and a house, and even a dog. - That was my plan and I told Coco excitedly. My mom asked me to be quiet, but was interrupted by Coco's job offer. Turns out, he owned a beauty salon right next to the cafe where we were. He told her that if she wanted it, the job was hers, because of my references. My mom's face changed. I think she realized that by judging people without knowing them, she could limit the blessings God had for her life. Through Coco we were able to discover that the love of God is manifested in different ways and through different people; that each of us has a life of sin and that it is up to us, with our love, to be a balm instead of a pounding rod.

> "Choose to be a *balm* that covers instead of a pounding rod."

Coco was five years in our life. The disease knocked on his door and very soon he was going to accompany my Daddy to a new place. But the years that God allowed him to be with us were a great blessing. Coco was the person who provided us with our first apartment.

He withdrew $200 from my mom's salary to pay for that small apartment where we lived our first 5 years here. It was a small 350 square foot place. My mom and I shared the bed, the dresser, what was seen on television ... everything. It was our beautiful miniature mansion. When Coco left this world, he gave us his humble house and put it in the name of both of us. He gave us his car and left the business papers in my mom's name. No one before had blessed us so much. My dad never thought of death as a possibility and we had no inheritance from him. However, this unknown named Coco left his entire inheritance to us, everything.

Now I think of him and marvel at the goodness of God. Coco was abused as a child and rejected by his family for his obvious mannerisms. Incredibly early he discovered that this abuse left him with a disease that would lead to death. Uncertainty, loneliness, and confusion were a constant struggle. He faced his pain with his sense of humor and infectious joy. He battled himself and his feelings, and he dedicated himself to giving love to everyone, as he would have liked to receive it. He was able to continue spreading the destructive disease, so he chose to be alone. He set about making each of his days filled with laughter. He dedicated himself to give his all in everything.

That night in a hospital bed, my mom and I were holding Coco's hands. A tall, passive, smiling man came up to us and asked if he could pray for our friend. Coco opened his eyes surprisingly like someone who sees a ray of hope in a very dark night, and replied:

-Please, Pastor, do it. - I had never heard the word "pastor". I did not know what he meant. We did not regularly attend any church, but on special occasions we went to mass. What happened at that time was of great impact to my life. The pastor asked Coco if he wanted to make a confession of faith. Coco answered yes and started crying like never before. Tears ran down my cheeks. I was 12 years old and I was witnessing one of the most significant moments of my life. I did not hesitate to take out my notebook, with which I always carried with me, and began to document what was happening. Coco asked God to please forgive his sins, and shouted:

-"Lord, I love you, Lord, I love you." I wrote in my notebook the words that the pastor said to him, which Coco repeated. - Write my name in the book of life - I heard him say. What book will that be? I remember wondering. Coco's face transformed before our eyes. A peace that I had never known before overwhelmed us all. Coco left us that night, but he left us so much!

I have learned that every human being has a story. Coco grew up in a Christian home and was marked by violence. People only saw one man who died of a disease that carries its own judgment. They judged not only him, but us for hanging out with him. That man all he did was take care of us as a remarkably close relative. He became family. He was made by decision my uncle. We inherited not only his humble and warm home, his business, and his car, we also inherited his neighborly love and his optimism . He also left something in us that we had never seen before. He gave us the faith to know that there was something more. That God was forgiving. That there was a Lord and Savior of our lives and a book in which we could, if we wanted, be enrolled in. That being that, God could flood an entire room with peace and was able to restore the lost gaze of a dying man.

The sound at the door announced the expected arrival of my friends Sandra and Luis.

-What a joy to see you again! Meet my mom, Naomi, and my daughter, Penelope Sofia-, I said with great joy in my voice as if I had known them for a lifetime. They came accompanied by his brother Raúl, his wife Laura and his niece Catalina. The girl was just 2 years older than my PitaSofía. Soon we started sharing while my mom served the food. Something beautiful happens in this country when you meet brothers who come from different Hispanic countries; automatically we are all family. Our language unites us in such a way that it makes all differences disappear. We speak differently, but we understand each other. Without thinking we shake hands and hug. That night was special. My mom was so happy. It was like meeting old friends or brothers. It was a family night that began a magical season in our lives.

> "Our *Father* knows what you need, before you ask Him."

- Pamela, come with us to the car. Come, everyone. - Luis said with special enthusiasm. We all went to the car, which was carrying a white wagon in the back. Upon opening the doors, the place carried not only the suitcases they brought from their trip for their new permanent stay, but there were several paddleboards. Luis carefully entered the cart and taking one of the boards in his arms he came out saying:

-Daughter, this board is a humble gift for you. It is a used board, a little battered, or let us say with a lot of experience on the sea. It is like you, pink and cheerful. It has some scars that do not affect its quality at all. I want you to enjoy it and use it for training. My eyes were filled with emotion and disbelief. I covered my mouth with my hands to my amazement. My daughter ran to hug me and said such wise words ... - See, mommy? Our Father knows what you need, before you ask Him.

"Even with scars and wounds, I must continue and *walk* on the water."

Each of the scars on the board was a reminder of the price Jesus paid for me on Calvary's cross. They also symbolized my life, my blows, my stumbles, my walk. But even with scars, that paddle board rendered its services. Even with scars and wounds, I must continue and walk on the water.

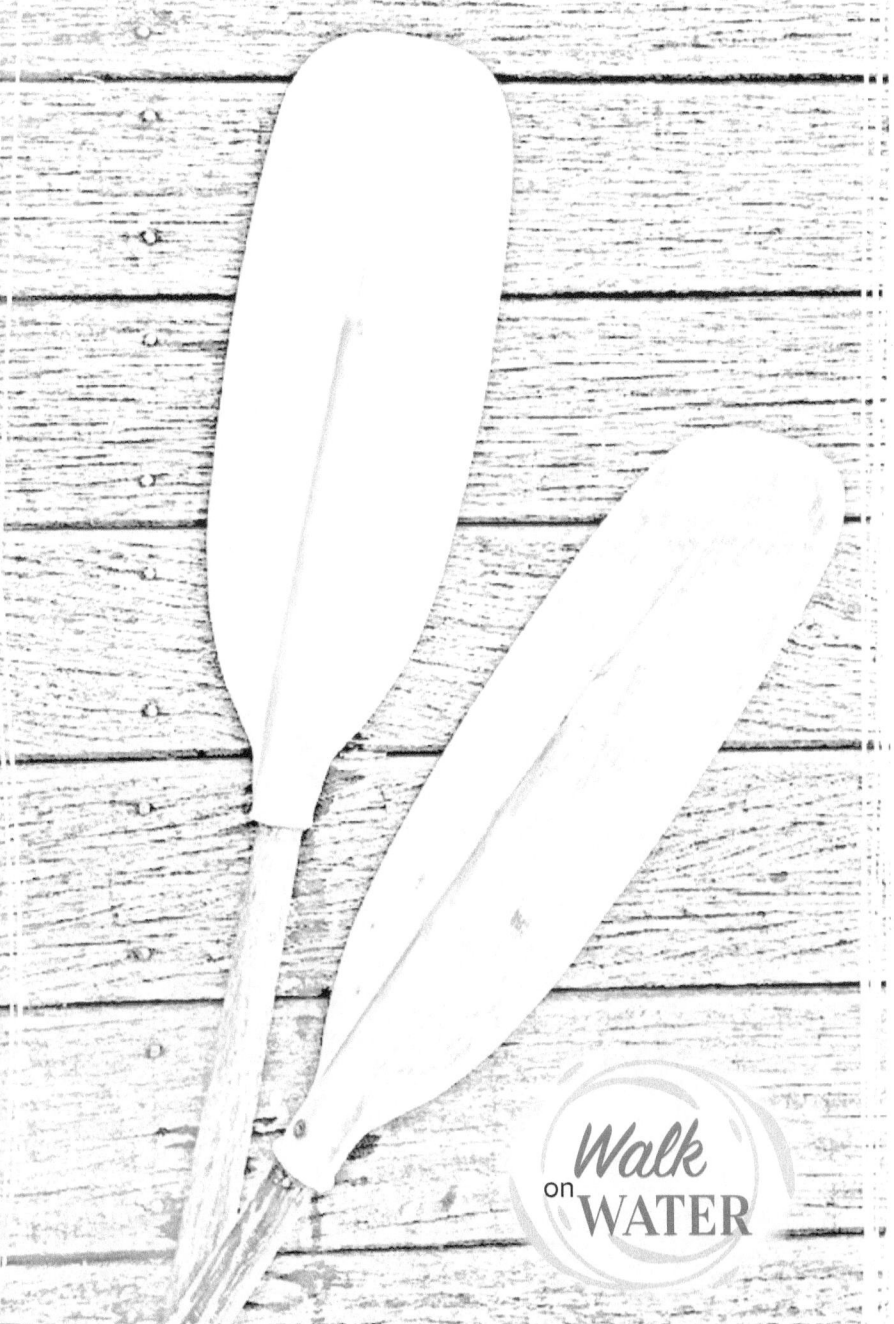

Chapter

11

Mom's advice:
Rest on the paddleboard

*"My child listen when your father corrects you.
Do not neglect your mother's instruction. What
you learn from them will crown you with grace
and be a chain of honor around your neck."*

(PROVERBS 1:8-9)

Every single person should have at least
a year of intimacy with Jesus before
starting to meet another person.

Elisa Jardo

It is early Saturday morning and we are going to spend
a family day and use for the first time my paddle board.
My mom and daughter are going with me. Today the

beauty salon took second place, Naomi will go with me to conquer the sea. I have always called my mom by name, Naomi. Since I have the use of reason it has been so. I remember my dad calling her and I repeated everything he said. She has always been serene, gave timely advice and that suitable help; she was that for my dad and it is for me today. She always knows which way to go, even though she needs a bit of company to get started. She is braver than she thinks and stronger than everyone imagines. But her fortress has a covering of sweetness that enchants everyone who knows her. We arrived at the beach early to get a good spot. Sandra, Luis, and their family will be there with their board rental business. It is a genuinely nice beach, 30 minutes from our home. I have a blue truck, the deep color of the sea. It was given to me by my ex-husband at some point in our failed marriage. It is the only thing I have from him and to be honest, I love it. In the back I have enough space to place my new board and it is ideal for this new hobby.

"Give yourself the opportunity to embrace your maternity and your identity."

When we got to the beach, we were located near the rental point for maritime sports equipment owned by Raúl, Luis's brother, "Walk in Water".

"Let's not wait too long, all the women are going to jump into the water," I yelled excitedly. Catalina and my Penelope Sofía were happy that they would use a paddle board together. I was happy to use mine.

- Not so fast, kids - Luis said with his nice accent. I want to say a prayer for everyone before we start the adventure. We all stopped. I forgot that Luis is a man of great faith and does not move if he does not pray. "Father, we present this day to you. We thank you for my brother Raúl and his family, who have blessed us by letting us work with them in their business. We declare harvest times. Father, we ask you for each one of the people who will be in the water today enjoying a beautiful day, that you take care of them, but above all, that you show Yourself. Let everything you do on the board, or even resting in front of the sea, be a deep learning experience. I ask this in the name of your beloved son Jesus, amen." We all said Amen.

-Luis, is that always the prayer you say before starting your workday on the board rental? - I asked intrigued ...- Yes, daughter, every day I pray that God reveals Himself to the people who rent from me the boards.

-Now I understand it all. When I rented your board in Aruba for the first time, I had a beautiful encounter with God. He spoke to my heart in everything that happened that day on the water. - I commented.

The day was perfect, a radiant sun was beginning to appear like a ray of hope to a new season that was about to begin.

- Naomi, what are you doing looking for a place to sit? Come with us to the water. - Since my dad died, she is overly cautious with the sea and I do not blame her. But to my great surprise, she said to me:

- I am going with you, but we need to share your board, I will not go alone to the sea.

I almost fell in surprise, but I think there must be great courage within that prudent heart. At the end of the day, if we are in this country it was thanks to her bravery. God has certainly sustained us, but my mom has been a very hard-working woman. We entered the water hugging, while Raúl gently brought us our board. The years have passed, but my mother has not aged. Next year she will be 50 and looks as young as ever. She has been a rock to me; she put her life on hold to take care of us. I never saw my mom set her eyes on another man. On multiple occasions I have recommended her to do so, but she has not listened to me. Although being very honest, I do not think I am prepared to see my mom loving someone other than my Daddy. But it is not about me, nor about him, but about her being happy. I think she has that gift of abstinence; she is that virtuous, very centered, and strong woman. She gives that timely advice in times of need.

"Do not help *God*."

God has surrounded me with wise women. Both my daughter and my mom have been positioned by God in my life with a purpose. I want someday to have the virtues that she possesses. I have lived my life like that little rabbit behind the carrot. Hearing that my daughter is ashamed has really made me reflect a lot. Happiness escapes me and I no longer know what direction to take, what should I try, what is the new strategy that I should focus on.

-Well, daughter, we are going to use this board as it should. To rest.

-For what? You have gone crazy, Naomi, let us practice, go ahead.

-No. I will put my arms on the board, I will lean on it and I will stretch my legs in the sea to feel its caresses. You do the same from your side. I used to do this with your dad. - She said the magic words. - Did you do this with daddy? You never told me.

> "Use this time to become the ideal woman, so when the ideal man arrives, he finds you in *plenitude* and not in necessity."

- There are many things that I have decided not to remember. It is part of being able to heal. But there is something in my heart that I want to share with you.

-Oh, oh, when you give me that introduction you come with a bomb.

- I was really intrigued.

- I know that you took those days in Aruba last month to think about what happened with Manuel and look for a new north. I want to invite you that this new north is not a man.

-Oh, Naomi, are you like Penelope Sofia? Are we going to start? - I invite you to give yourself the time to meet Jesus. I invite you to give yourself the opportunity to embrace your singleness, your motherhood and your identity, Pamela. I want to invite you to take this time to become the ideal woman so that when that man arrives, he finds you fully complete and not in need. Let that person be brought into your life by God and give yourself the opportunity to grow so that you can be ready to receive him.

> "Every single person should give themselves at least a year being intimate with *Jesus* before entering a new relationship."

-But how is that going to happen? Do not tell me he is going to knock on my door.

-I do not know, but that does not matter today. What matters is that you are healthy, ready. Give yourself a year without looking at anyone. Do that challenge. The pastor says that every single person should have at least a year of intimacy with Jesus before starting to meet another person.

-A year, Naomi? I am going to be almost 30. Do you want me to stay single?

-I want you to stop feeling rushed, because the rush led to three broken relationships, many illusions of grandeur, leaving you a broken woman and having a confused daughter.

-Embarrassed, you will say. - They are the consequences. It is up to you. There is time for everything in life... Ecclesiastes 3 - Everything has its time in this life. Give yourself a year without looking at anyone. Do not help God.

I was stunned listening to my mom's words. It was not the first time I received them, but it was the first time that my ears heard them audibly. They were certainly the words that echoed in my heart all day long from God. It was God Himself using my mom with infinite wisdom to tell me what I needed to hear. That wise advice at the right time. My mom kept saying ...

-You have spent your life looking for that ideal man and you have not dedicated a penny of your time to becoming that virtuous woman who deserves that ideal man. I am not saying that you are not a great woman. I know you deserve a wonderful man in your life and this is why I invite you to stop. Pause at the rhythm of your life. Dedicate yourself to falling in love with Jesus. Dedicate yourself to conquer the love of God. Dedicate yourself to perfecting the virtue that God has placed in you. Dedicate yourself to knowing yourself, to knowing God's purposes for your life. Once you reach yourself, you will be up to achieving what you have been created for. Not before. If you continue in this search race, you will continue to fail.

"Naomi ..." I tried to persuade her to stop, but it was impossible.

> "You have spent your life looking for that ideal man and you have not dedicated a penny of your time to becoming that *virtuous woman* who deserves that ideal man."

-Your eyes are not ready to discern the right person. And when you are not healthy, your character is not healthy, and you cannot be molded to deal with difficult situations. Without identity you will not be grounded in Christ to endure battles and to appreciate victories in marriage. Wait to be ready and you will see the difference, and you will remember this conversation. There is time for adventures at sea and there is time to stop a little and meditate on the board. Give yourself a year. Listen to your mother's advice.

"There is time for *adventures* on the ocean but there are also times to stop and meditate on the board."

When my mom finished, I could only jump on the board trying to hug her like that little 5-year-old girl who had lost her dad and needed her mom immensely. This girl who lost her north and who was here faced with a reality that needed to be said and heard. I received my mother's advice knowing that came from a pure and upright heart, and that it has the sole intention of protecting me. And I said yes. I will wait, I will give myself that year she asked for.

Rest

12

On the

potter's wheel

"But the vessel that he was making of clay was spoiled in the hand of the potter; so, he remade it into another vessel, as it pleased the potter to make."

JEREMIAH 18:4

Could have discarded me but chose me.

Elia Hando

My life has been taking an unexpected turn. Now I spend a lot of time with my mom and daughter, and it has been a beautiful season. I have a new family with Luis and Sandra, who more than being my paddle board coaches, are my friends and more than friends, they have become spiritual parents.

Catalina, Luis and Sandra's niece and my daughter spend time together and that has been wonderful and Lisa ... Lisa came into my life as an angel of God. God put her in my way because how else could I meet this Argentine woman full of gifts. She has a contagious joy in those 4 feet 8 inches that does not do justice to her inner greatness. Lisa is a clinical psychologist and I decided to start therapy with her when problems in my past marriage began to drag me into depression. She first spoke to me about narcissistic personality disorder, and made me understand the cycle of emotional abuse I was in. But more than anything, Lisa became my friend, my older sister. The one I always wanted to have.

I met her on my first visit to the church when I ended my relationship with José and she tried, like so many others, to prevent me from marrying Manuel, but I ignored her. With her I have learned so much! She has a phrase that distinguishes her and that I have made it mine: "No one can stop a woman who, even with tears in her eyes, walks." That phrase fills me with strength and determination. It was she who recommended that I go to Aruba for a few days to reflect after my divorce, and we have talked so much about my experiences on the paddle board that I wanted to invite her.

> "No one can stop a woman who, even with tears in her eyes, *walks.*"

-My friend, I am leaving my house, I will go to you first and from there we will pick up Sandra and Luis. What do you think?

- Done, friend, I already finished getting ready. Just come over and we can go at once for an adventure. - Her Argentine accent always seems so festive; it seems that she speaks in colors.

Sandra and Luis chose a beautiful river with very temperate waters, spectacular. You can see every leaf, every fish ... I hope only that, and not an alligator. Here in Florida you never know.

-Daughters, this will be an experience of great reflection. Take time to reflect on your lives, just as the water allows you to see your reflection on it. This will be a calm experience, without fighting against the wind, without waves and with great peace because there is no wind. - Luis commented.

-When he finished speaking, Luis got down on his knees on his board, Sandra accompanied him and us, of course, also. Three other people we met accompanied us on the tour. Luis made his habitual prayer and they stood up. I had gotten on my knees just like them, but I did not finish when they did. The truth is that I do not know if they left fast, or if I extended myself in my prayer. The reality is that the experience I had that day did not allow me to continue.

I was on my knees on the paddle board, as were the others. My board was on the grass, I had not yet put it into the water. I put my head between my knees to say a short prayer and I wanted to ask God to give me an experience on that day. A peace began to flood me terribly. It was a feeling like no other. I did not want it to stop. I quickly started to feel a weight on my back that was becoming so real it was impossible to ignore it. It was solid but refreshing and invigorating as the best of massages. I did not want to stop that experience. The best way I can describe it is as a presence. But to think that I could be experiencing the presence of God made me cry, crying out from within "I don't deserve it."

Tears of pain from the bottom of my heart flowed non-stop as I thought: Why me? Why myself? I could not describe it, but I knew I did not deserve to be living an experience like this. But there was something more, something more intense still happened. It really happened. I had the feeling that someone had pushed a button and suddenly everything started to spin. And I do not mean the outside world, it was me. Well, I did not know if I was physically moving or not. But I was certain that I was going around in one place. It is the best way I can explain it. It was a supernatural experience that I had not experienced before. I wanted it to stop, but at the same time I wanted it to continue. While I was in that experience I wondered where the others would be. I do not know how long I was there, long enough to be exhausted. When I opened my eyes, I realized that I was in the same place. I never moved. What happened? As I sat up, I heard Lisa's voice say to me:

"God is going to apply pressure, it is not a pressure that destroys but *creates*."

150

-And what were you thinking, friend, did you forget our marathon? - she said with her sense of humor.

-Oh, Lisa, something so strange just happened to me. I do not even know how to explain.

- I started trying to explain it in words, but the sensations require so much vocabulary or knowing how to draw. I am not incredibly good at explaining my emotions when speaking.

Lisa interrupted me and she gave me a look, like she has experienced what was happening to me before.

-Weight of Glory, friend, you have experienced the weight of the Glory of Jehovah.

-What? - I asked intrigued.

-That is it my friend, look no further. God allowed you to experience His Glory from this place.

- Lisa, why me? Why me? How does He allow me to feel this experience? I do not deserve anything. I have only made mistakes. I am not a faithful servant of Him, I am a sinner and I am so unfaithful that at the first temptation I run away for a new adventure.

-This is God. I started to explain about the button, how I felt going around in circles. I wanted to know if I was really moving or not. She says I did not move a a bit. But I felt myself moving inside.

-Friend, you were at the potter's wheel. Do you know what that means? The potter's wheel. God has begun his work in you. You were not moving outside at all. You were still out here, but inside God is doing something great. Great friend, it is great.

My tears rolled down my cheeks and a mixture of vulnerability with gratitude dominated my being.

-I did not leave, because I felt that you needed me here. I knew something was up, but of course I was not going to imagine what it could be. His hands began to mold the clay with intensity, but gently and delicately. He is building a great vessel, sister, that is you - Lisa said to me with emotion. At this point we were both crying.

-Oh, Lisa, now I do not know if the crazy person is me or is it you. - We crack up. An incessant joy made us laugh at any nonsense.

-It is the touch of the Spirit, Pamelita. The Holy Spirit plays.

Lisa was married to a very tall Guatemalan man, a lawyer, and a university professor. They came noticeably young to this country and fell in love at the university. They had been together for many years and had recently adopted a child. They were that couple that everyone wants to be. Like-minded, professional, successful, believers, faithful. They had walked in purity before they were married and modeled others with their testimony and love story. Lisa was small in stature, but incredibly wise, and she had a laugh so loud it made her contagious. She is one of those people who has an insightful comment for everything that happens.

"It is *time* to become the woman you want to be and leave behind the broken girl."

-Pamela ... - When she begins a prayer with my name, she is going to say something strong, something I must listen to ... - God is calling you to a time of rest. The potter immobilizes the piece with his hands so that he can work it. He is going to put on pressure. It is not a pressure that destroys but creates. This is your time to stay still and recover. Furthermore, it is time to get to know yourself, and to enjoy what God is creating in you. It is time to know your Creator deeply. It is time to become the woman you want to be and leave behind the broken girl. He already took the clay, put water on it and began to form it. He has already turned on the lathe. This is the time to be rebuilt. You are at the potter's table. Only He can straighten your steps. I can advise you; I can analyze you and give you recommendations, but I cannot change you. Only God transforms. You are an imperfect woman loved by a perfect God. It is just that.

> "You are an imperfect woman, *loved* by a perfect God."

Lisa began to describe the potter's wheel in detail. She explained to me how the potter takes the clay that is worth nothing and decides to place fresh water on it. Then with his hands he begins to mold it and once it has given it a little shape, he places it on the lathe and on that wheel, he begins to massage that vessel. The potter gives you the height, width, and

> "He could have rejected me, but He *choose me.*"

depth that He determines, depending on what He wants to use that pot for later. The clay is left to be molded by the potter because He is the artist who knows how to create art from the earth.

God, like a potter, that morning had shown me that He had decided to take me, a dirty and useless piece of clay, put fresh living water on me and began to remold me. The potter had turned his wheel to work on me. It meant so much to me to know that He found me capable of being molded, that He thought of me that I could be a vessel with height, width, and depth as to receive its precious deposit. That I could be used. That I could be an important piece in His collection. He could have discarded me, but he chose me. I knew that I had been on the potter's wheel and something in me had changed. I had a lot to ponder, I had a lot to write tonight and there was no time to lose. This afternoon it was necessary to write this great teaching.

blog

My Board of Salvation

Today I was at the potter's wheel and I understood that:

- I am valuable to God even if the world has rejected me.

- I can be transformed; go from being clay to a beautiful vessel.
- The potter can give me height. I can recover that dignity that I have lost. That virtue that I feel I never had, only He can offer it to me.
- The potter can give me the width. I can expand to new possibilities that I never thought of. God will determine how much space I must cover, where I can go, what will be the purpose of my life, how far I will extend.
- The potter is giving me depth. To understand the greatness of His name, he is making me deep. To connect my spirit with His, he is entering His hand inside me and creating a space of depth for his spirit to inhabit.
- I understood that although I do not deserve it, He has made me worthy. That although I have no courage, He has called me capable. That although I have done nothing to deserve it, He has chosen me.

If this teaching has touched your heart, share it on your social networks under #Myboardofsalvation

 SHARE

13

Forgiveness... in the crocodile's canal

*"If you forgive those who sin against you,
your heavenly Father will forgive you."*

MATTHEW 6:14

I forgive the one I was, I accept the one I
am, and I receive the one I will be.

Elia Ilardo

Saturday morning, ready for a great day to go with
my friends to a new adventure in paddleboarding.
The destination, the canals of Venice in Winter Park.
A place with landscapes that look like something
out of a postcard, the water is crystal clear, lush
ancient trees are everywhere, and the flowers in the
gardens of traditional Victorian houses are worthy of
appreciation. Almost four hours to get there, but it

is worth the trip. We arrive full of expectation at the park that borders the lake.

-Pamela, Lisa, I want you to know that this tour that we will take today will take us through beautiful canals covered in exuberant beauty that you have never seen before. Then we will go out to a very wide area that looks like a beautiful Caribbean beach ... But do not get confused, it is a lake. - Luis told us.

-How do you know so much about Florida, Luis? - I asked curious. -I spent a long season in Orlando a few years ago trying to get my residency. At that time, it was not possible to achieve it, it was not the time. I returned to my land, Venezuela, and since God's times are perfect, the opportunity was given now to return thanks to the help of my brother Raúl.

We prayed on the shore and the four of us left, each with a paddle board. It had been several months since we went out to practice paddle board because their business was taking up a lot of time. We were already entering October and the temperatures are no longer so attractive for many people to go to the beach. So, Sandra and Luis have more time for these adventures in the water.

The wind did not favor us, we were fighting to advance, and Luis had a significant advantage. Soon we began to see that a narrow path awaited us to our left to give us rest. It was one of the channels that we had heard about. Houses on either side protected the beautiful canal and majestic flower-covered trees gave it an exquisite shade that seemed to hug us. Paddling on our boards in these narrow channels we could enjoy the backyards of the houses with a colorful variety of flowers. Luis interrupted my autumn postcard with information that in no way brought me peace.

- Pamela, stay away from the shore of the channel because that is where the alligators hide.

- Alligators? Are you kidding me, Luis?

-No, girl, not at all. Anywhere in Florida where there is water can have alligators and crocodiles. And the channels are famous for being a place where they hide.

-Thanks for the information, Luis, you should have told me in Miami. Look, I did not come to die in Winter Park.

-We laughed with my sarcasm.

-Pamela, you better play dumb and do not ask any more questions. I do not want to know anything else. I do not want to have more information, since I am in this problem. Look, today I will charge you for the consultation, my dear. - Added Lisa with her funniest Argentine accent that is sharpened when she is nervous.

Her comment obviously terrified us, but we humorously dealt with the challenge.

We continue paddling now focused on looking at the center and watching the corners. There was 3 feet of distance between the center and each side of the canal. It was better to traverse the romantic canals at full speed.

As we continued to move forward, Lisa made a comment full of wisdom.

-Pamelita, that is the way life is. We must stay in the center, keeping ourselves in balance and away from the extremes.

-You are right, doctor - replied Luis. -When we lead a disordered life and when we go to extremes, we expose ourselves and put our lives at risk. - We make mistakes, right, Luis. Lisa replied.

-Very true, doctor, the people who live on the edge, do not know what kind of alligators they can face.

All this conversation made me reflect. That was me until just a few months ago. All my life living on the edge, in the extremes, always close to danger, always with some alligator lurking. But not anymore. Now I want a safe life, a dignified life, I want a centered life. I truly hope that my daughter is proud of me. May my mom rest her nerves and be happy? I want God to find me ready for Him. But suddenly, before my astonished eyes, that small channel came to an end, a beautiful wide view as of an ocean made its way before our eyes. It was a great giant circle, like a bay. It really looked like an ocean. The wide and crystalline view produced a peace and spoke to me of a future. Of a hope, of a way out. Of an unexpected potential that exceeded all my expectations.

> "*Pain* can blur our vision and we are at risk of making wrong departures."

-What is this beautiful place? - I exclaimed spontaneously. I began to reflect on how we sometimes go through seasons so difficult, so narrow, so dangerous, so harmful, and so suffering that we believe that it will be like this permanently. Pain mists our gaze and we are at risk of making wrong starts and decisions. Only the grace of God can keep us at the center. And suddenly when we least think about it, we enter a new season, a large space. That is the season I know I am going to enter. Isaiah 43:19 came to my mind: "Behold, I will do something new, now it will spring forth; will you not be aware of it? I will even make a roadway in the wilderness, rivers in the desert."

-Let's go to the center, to the heart of this lake, and sit on our boards. We are going to enjoy the beauty of God's creation. - Luis said.

The spaciousness that my eyes saw represented the possibilities of my future. I had never looked at my future with greater possibilities or with faith. I pondered the possibility that circumstances might be better for me, but tears ran down my cheeks at that thought. Lisa approached me with her board, she held my board with her paddle to make me look at her, and looking at me with a palpable sweetness, but a penetrating intensity, she asked me: - Why are you crying, sister?

-I do not know. I want to believe in a future, but it is hard for me. I find it hard to believe. - I replied.

-Pamela, look at me, did you forgive your father? What did she just say? I looked at her incredulously. Forgive my father? I searched my mind for a quick answer, a logical answer to such an absurd question.

But my heart in a microsecond compressed like a little raisin. Like a dry sponge I became nothing. I started crying with the deepest pain I could ever feel. Screams of pain came out. Sandra and Luis looked at me with tenderness, and I know that they interceded in prayer.

Something broke. I screamed in pain. Knowing that no one else was hearing me, I let it out: "Why did you leave me, Daddy?" Why did you abandon me? Why didn't you stay here? With me! With mom! - I felt arms on my back trying to comfort me. I felt a horrible cold in my body, but an intense heat inside. I never felt anything like it. I never thought those feelings were inside of me. I was never aware of them until today. The retaining wall that held those waters of pain broke. Consciousness began to come to me as I calmed down.

I reflected, all my life I felt that he abandoned me, he left me alone, forcing me to grow amazingly fast. I know it was an accident, but I lived in a world of confusion. I did not want to recognize how much I needed him, and I made so many mistakes trying to fill that space, that emptiness. Everything seemed foolish on my part; So, I never accepted those feelings. But it was the internal scream of a girl who sometimes fantasized that perhaps he was in some country of the world enjoying life while we missed him. That maybe he never died, that maybe he just abandoned us and did not have the courage to tell us. Today I remember that sometimes when I cried, I would dry my tears with courage because I imagined him alive and in another place that was not with me. And regardless of whether that place was heaven or the arms of another family, I was angry to know that he was somewhere else and that he was not here.

-You have opened a box to which you had never allowed access. Do not stop there, Pamela. There is more to come - Lisa approached me. She began listing each of the people whom I had to forgive. And I started to declare:

I forgive Alberto for taking advantage of my innocence, for having betrayed my love and for having stolen my purity. I admit that I gave him the opportunity but I accept that I was the victim of a person who took advantage of my tender age and committed an illegal act. I forgive him for abandoning his daughter, my daughter, for never taking care of her, for not even coming to meet her. I forgive him for his infamy and let him go. I forgive José for rejecting me, for having seen me as less than him. I forgive him for not choosing me, for making me feel marked. I forgive him because even his gentleness and chivalry hurt me. For his thoughts that caused me pain, I forgive him. I forgive him for choosing another person that he considered better than me. I forgive him and let him go. I forgive Manuel for having hurt me so much with his words, for having been so hard, for having broken in me the illusion of a marriage. I forgive him for his lies, for his narcissism, I forgive him for having promised to be a family man, a provider, and a protector. I forgive him for not knowing how to be a good stepfather for my daughter. I forgive him because he tore my heart apart with each of his harsh words and his intimidation. I forgive him for his emotional abuse. I forgive him and let him go.

But the list continued. God brought people to my mind that I did not think I should forgive.

I forgive my mom for not being a leader, stronger, more independent. I forgive her because I know she did her best and has been a great mother to me. I thought it was over when Lisa told me:

- The most important forgiveness is missing, two are missing. Do you think you have to forgive God?
- What a difficult question! I recognize God as the creator of everything, however, I confess to you, Lisa, that sometimes deep inside I claimed... God, why didn't I meet you before? Why didn't you rescue me in my childhood? Why not? Did you rescue my father? Why didn't you protect me from Alberto? Why didn't you warn me about José? Why didn't you avoid that wedding? But the reality is that each of those were human decisions, some of them mine. I do not think I have a right to forgive God. God does not deserve that I do not even think about Him like that.

-Very well, she replied, but you have someone left - I looked at her strangely and she told me. - This is perhaps the most difficult of pardons, but you must do it to be free. Are you able to forgive yourself? I looked at her in shock, thinking, what are you talking about? But a pain in my soul confirmed that this is the forgiveness I needed to say the most.

- You're right, Lisa, that is the most difficult of all. How can I forgive myself? I spent all my life secretly hating my Daddy for leaving. I used all my energy to be in control of my house and to do what I wanted. I used my influence to get my mom to let me do whatever I wanted. I keep calling her by her first name to avoid submitting to her authority. I was a rebel disguised as a leader. I was willing, but I dressed as a person with great initiative.

I looked for Alberto when he did not even look at me, I was making eyes at him when he tried to let me pass, I provoked him. I went after José knowing that I should focus on being a young mother. I gave my heart to him at the wrong time and gave myself no courage. I gave him my daughter's heart, without right. I gave myself so cheap. Then I went out with the face of a victim to console myself in the arms of a man full of chauvinism and narcissism. I sought my punishment. I got into the wolf's mouth.

My mom warned me many times: "Don't marry him." What happened to me I looked for. I have been so foolish; I cannot forgive myself. I cried for several minutes. Lisa was just watching. In silence she accompanied me and passed her hand along my back. The three of them approached my board, surrounded me, and placed their arms on me. They had created a human bond and lulled me. It was such a special moment; I heard their voices whispering to a lullaby. I felt so special, so loved.

An explosion of love began to erupt from within me. It started with a brief awareness of how great God's mercy is. I could see myself with the love and tenderness that He saw me. I was able to forgive myself and empathize with myself. I saw myself as He saw me; I was no longer that girl. I could see myself from another perspective. In my confusion I made many mistakes, but my heart simply sought the love of a father. I could understand that life is simply hard, and we do not always know how to act in certain situations. I forgive the one I was, accept the one I am and receive the one I will be.

I understood that this is a new beginning, a new chapter, and a new opportunity for me. I forgive myself because I did not know what I was doing. And now that I know and have discovered what God is doing in me, I forgive myself and give myself the opportunity to start again. Today begins a new life for Pamela.

blog

This day I learned ...

- That we must stay close to Him and stay away from dangerous extremes that bring us horrible dangers.

- That no matter how ugly or narrow the path you are going through now; you can always go out into a large and comforting space.
- That when we decide to forgive is when we open ourselves to the freedom of crystal-clear water. That forgiving others is as important as forgiving ourselves.
- That if you fell into the alligator's mouth it was not just because he wanted to, but because you got too close.
- That you can always start a new purpose, a new path, and a new opportunity for yourself, if you are able to leave the past behind and enjoy your present.

Today I forgive the one I was, I accept the one I am, and I receive the one I will be.

If this teaching has touched you, please share it on your social networks under #Myboardofsalvation

 SHARE

Chapter
14
I walked with Jesús; and fell *in love*

"My lover said to me, Rise up, my darling! Come away with me, my fair one! Look, the winter is past, and the rains are over and gone. The flowers are springing up, the season of singing birds has come, and the cooing of turtledoves fills the air. The fig trees are forming young fruit, and the fragrant grapevines are blossoming. Rise up, my darling! Come away with me, my fair one!"

SONG OF SOLOMON 2:10-13

I discovered that I would wait; because I do not need anything if I have Him, but I would lose everything if I have Him not.

Elia Jardo

I woke up early in the morning with a sweet voice in my ears saying:

- Get up, my beautiful - I jumped out of bed to the voice of my Beloved. I knew it was Jesus. A feeling of running to my beloved overwhelmed me. I needed to get out of my room, I wanted to receive him, give him my full attention. I sat on the floor in the living room of our humble home. We had a white sofa, old, but very faithful. It had endured Penelope's accidents, the affection of Coco's dog while he lived, and the occasional spilled coffee. The cushions and the turquoise blue carpet like the Caribbean Sea formed that small room where Jesus visited me with His love. I crossed my legs in front of me, hugged my pillow, confident that we would start a beautiful conversation. My Beloved and me.

An ecstasy of love began to flow from within me. A pure, sacred love, a tender love. This love makes me shed tears of joy and raises a song in me: Fall in love with you, Lord ...

-I do not know how to do it without you. I depend on you. I need you. In my strength I am weak. In my decisions I am foolish. In my wisdom I fall short. It is my need to listen to you. Guide me. Do not leave me alone, Jesus.

Time passed quickly, like when you are in love. Laughter, crying, songs, words, reading, writing ... It is an adventure every day with my beloved Jesus.

Lord, I want today to be my special day. Christmas is over,

"An eruption of *love* flows from within me. Make me fall in love with you, Lord."

Valentine's Day is coming up and I am ready for a love date. It is almost spring, and my birthday is approaching. I want my birthday today.

-I invite you -. That was his reply. Tears come out of my eyes upon hearing his tender voice. There is nothing that moves me as much as his breathing in me, his sweet voice, the voice of Jesus. I have started a relationship with God that has no comparison. I never imagined Him. Every morning in His presence is a new adventure; it is certainly a love relationship.

-Come on, daughter, get ready for a date with your Creator.

- Those were the words that God spoke to my heart. I did not think twice, I did not ask for confirmation. I jumped in my truck and drove without a destination, but in the direction of Fort Lauderdale, the East.

-Today we are going to do paddle boarding-. Those were the words that I felt God spoke to my heart.

-But, Lord, I did not bring my board.

-It does not matter, rent one. - Was His reply.

I managed to pull out on a busy avenue called Las Olas Boulevard, a small "vintage" truck where they rented boards. I parked my blue pickup and a young man who was not even 20 years old, long hair blond like the sun, attended me with much sweetness. He was the only one attending the station, so this time I had to carry the board to my starting place. It was not close at all, and these boards are heavy. He said it was half a mile, I think he lied, and it was a whole mile with a flavor of three. I do not want to take so much credit for myself, but I confess that while walking with that board I felt like Jesus carrying his cross. I had to make 10 to 20 stops to breathe and change the position of the board. I put the board on my side, over my head, on the other side, with one hand, with both hands ... Sometimes I usually spiritualize everything, I know, but I confess that I was looking for some Simon of Cyrene to offer me a hand. I can imagine Jesus laughing at my thoughts. In my opinion the weight was 120 pounds! Yes, I know I am an exaggerating. Well it was heavy! So, I say.

Anyway, I went to the marina area because it was closer than the beach, and when I got to the water, I already felt victimized by this society. I regretted feminism and any other type of female autonomy that has been eliminating along the way the wonderful gentlemen who could have offered me help. Hey, I am not a feminist or a bodybuilder! I was looking for someone to load my board, yes, that is the truth, and I already wanted to start crying. A little help for this skinny country girl from western Puerto Rico would have been fantastic. But, finally, to finish off my walk on the painful road, I fell on the ramp and scraped my knees. Now I must look so pretty, sarcasm included. Well, since they told me to stop flirting with everyone and to focus on Jesus, now there is no one to look at me with these 8-year-old girl's knees, sweaty and possibly not very fragrant. These brief internal conversations, thank goodness that they are not projected on a television. How powerful is the mind!

- Do you think your load is greater than mine was?

- that voice ... - I know that voice well. My heart started pounding. I already earned the first slap of the day for daring, comparing my load with that of Jesus. I knew that would be the beginning of an unforgettable conversation.

-Forgive me, Lord, you still have so much to do with me. This reconstruction is going to take time, please do not tire of me. - I answered Jesus inside me. I remember that voice since I was a child. I cannot say when it started, but somehow, I always knew it was the voice of God. Maybe someone explained it to me, I cannot remember. But he had always been with me. Sometimes its volume was exceptionally low, but sometimes, like today, it almost seemed audible. It was an incredibly wise voice to make His ideas mine, it was too fast to be my mind, and it was true, almost always contrary to what my mind said. It was a sublime voice and it came from within me, but it entered my heart from my ears. It was so clear that I can take it in writing. It was so different from

"Its was a *voice* too wise to be mine, it was too fast to be my thinking, and it was so truthful almost contrary to what my mind said. It was a sublime voice and it came from within me, but it entered my heart from my ears."

my thoughts that they can both speak at the same time. That voice was God. It was always God. That is my Jesus. Today is going to be a remarkably interesting day. I want to hear His voice, just His voice.

> "God makes my heart *smile*."

-Jesus, your yoke is easy, and your burden is light. My board does not compare with your cross, my knees are in no way like the scars on your body. I replied.

- Just checking, daughter, just checking. - Who says Jesus has no sense of humor? I love when Your voice speaks to me as I speak. He is so cool and so pure at the same time, how can he do it? He is God. He reaches me in my immaturity. He drops to my level of understanding and makes my heart smile.

-Today we are you and I, my beloved girl. Today I have a little training for you.

-Oh, oh ... it feels like it will be an interesting day ...

- Every day it is. - He replied without haste. - I want you to enter the water standing on the board. Do not start on your knees today. At least I avoided you a pain and I think you already knew that. Do not kneel for today.

- I can see his face smiling tenderly when saying this to me. Who is like Jesus?

-Thank you. - I replied. - I did not know how I would do it.

I put my board in the water, and used my paddle to draw it close. I placed my left foot on it, I took stock for a moment and went to put my right foot on the board... I do not know if it was a joke from the wind, but I fell into the water without anything prevented me.

In other words, I fell on the ramp and now the same people who saw me slip, now see me fall into the water. Really?

-No drama, daughter, it was just a little joke to refresh you.

- God, you provoke the most beautiful laughs inside me. - I love you God! Is this going to be like this all day? - I asked laughing, without waiting for an answer.

Nothing happened. It was barely 3 feet deep and I wiped the sweat off from the walk here. I felt a little ashamed and I was looking like a rookie enough of that for today, so I drew strength from where I did not have it. I pushed myself up with everything I had. I got on the board and I was on my feet in a second. Like an expert. I really wanted to impress.

"Bravo," were his next words. - that is my girl! - I smiled convinced that I had impressed Dad. I almost made a gesture of celebration.

I began to paddle, identifying everything around me and defining my route to follow. I wanted to discover new areas and was curious to get closer to the areas of millionaires' houses. I wanted to see their patios and dream that I lived in each one of them. But his strong voice stopped my plan.

- Where are you going, my daughter?

- Why, do you have any plans? Because I have some ideas.

- Ideas? Of those I have plenty. I have one for each day. In one week, I built a tremendous paradise. - Was his masterful response.

> "If you follow my voice, you will advance to a safe *destination*."

I smirked. - I want you to look from here to the very center of this marina. Identify which is the center. - he told me.

It would seem easy to identify the center, but once you are in the water the center changes position constantly. I went to it and as I got closer, I began to doubt if it was actually in the center or had I turned towards one of the banks somehow. I wanted to obey, but in the water, everything seems unstable, restless, movable.

-That's life, daughter. Unstable, restless, movable. What you see today is no longer tomorrow. The goals move with your walk and the only thing that remains is my voice. If you chase dreams, they will move to the rhythm of your paddle board. If you chase my voice, you will advance to a safe destination. Learn to listen and you will be wise in all your decisions. "Let the wise listen to these proverbs and become even wiser. Let those with understanding receive guidance." (Proverbs 1:5)

- Now, daughter, stop paddling. Those were His last words for the next two hours.

I asked - ... Jesus ... did you go to take care of another girl? Is there something going on in the world that needs you? Did you forget we were going for a walk? Where are you? Why silence? What do I do now? The silence drives me crazy. The absence.

In my two-hour monologue I said so much. I thought if I would just shut up for about two minutes then try again to convince Him to respond.

- The silence is going to make me go away -, I said insisting. This does not work for me, Jesus. Do not leave me here. I have a daughter.

- I tried everything and nothing. Two hours later I decided to lie down on the board and shut up. I should have decided to do that before. I had been standing for two hours waiting. I laid down and was silent for maybe 10, 20 or 30 minutes ... I do not know. I lost the sense of time. A peace flooded me. The satisfaction of stillness finally captivated my soul. At that time, I knew that I did not have to speak to say words. That I did not have to listen to receive instructions. That I did not have to move to go forward.

- Daughter, you just must learn to wait so you can enjoy the wait.

-Lord, I read that book, "The Value of Waiting" by Stephanie Campos, nice, but I did not think we were coming here to wait ... but on an adventure ...

-Daughter, the healthy wait. While you wait things happen, things that you do not see. In your waiting you calm down. Your skin matured in your wait in the sun, just as your soul does. When you walk with me you will see that the waiting is still "action". Stand up and paddle, I want you to see the way. The time for action has arrived. I got up to paddle and I cannot explain how it happened. I was right behind the millionaires' houses!

But when did we move there? It was right in the center of the marina exit. Far from everything, close to nothing. When and how did I get here?

- Delight yourself in me and I will grant you the wishes of your heart.

-It is Psalm 34:7, I know it very well, it is one of my favorites. Both that one and this one that says: "Yet I am confident I will see the Lord's goodness while I am here in the land of the living." (Psalm 27:13)

-Daughter, that verse continues saying: "Wait patiently for the Lord. Be brave and courageous. Yes, wait patiently for the Lord."

- "When you go through deep waters, I will be with you. When you go through rivers of difficulty, you will not drown. When you walk through the fire of oppression, you will not be burned up; the flames will not consume you." (Isaiah 43:2)

. . . .

"Today / *discover* that I will wait because I do not need anything if I have Him, but I will lose everything if He is not with me. "

. . . .

178

blog

Today I lived a very romantic afternoon. Verses of love came from His lips one after another. I felt like a bride dressed for marriage. Discovering the love of Jesus was healing every insecurity I had and every doubt of a future for my life. While looking at the luxurious houses, I no longer imagined living in them, my vision had changed. I could see the waters and imagine myself walking on the streets of pure gold like crystal that the Bible describes in Revelation 21:21. The beautiful mansions that Jesus went to build us. That afternoon I fell completely in love with Jesus. There I confirmed 5 things:

- That I do not want anything without Him. I discovered that if I must leave Him to be with a partner, I prefer to be alone and serve Him.
- I came to the certainty that if I ever have an opportunity to be in love again, he must be a man given by God and not wanted by me.
- I want someone who is like Him. May his love phrases sound like Jesus's, may his voice remind me of the one I have heard today. May his treatment be soft, like the one Jesus gives me.

- I want his love to remind me of Your love. May our hearts beat at the speed of Jesus, like a single song.
- I want an imitator of Jesus on this earth, I want to see Jesus in my beloved, or I want nothing. Today I fell in love. Today I discovered love in Jesus. Today I discovered that I would wait because I do not need anything if I have Him, but I would lose everything if I have Him not.

If this message helps you, touches you, edifies you or can help someone else, please share it on your social networks under #Myboardofsalvation

 SHARE

Chapter

15

Meet my true *Father*

*"The Lord is like a father to his children, tender
and compassionate to those who fear him."*

(PSALMS 103:13)

When we believed we were alone, we were
resting on a lifeline that was His hands.

Elisa Jardo

This morning I woke up so tired. I went to my prayer
corner in the living room and did nothing but fall
asleep. I struggled with sleep and tried to adore him.
It was Saturday, the week had been so busy. Today
I was going out with my daughter and my friends,
Sandra, and Luis to another adventure on the paddle
board. But I was tired. I work from Monday to Friday,
and on Saturdays I wish I could stay in my bed later,
but I do not want to miss my mornings in the presence
of Jesus. I fell asleep for minutes and when I woke

up, I began to ask the Lord for forgiveness. I was so embarrassed because I had not been able to stay awake to pray as I had agreed. Suddenly a vision began to flow. God speaks to me in visions in an incredibly special way. As if I were putting a gigantic television screen in front of my eyes. Regardless of whether my eyes are open or closed, I can see it, and it does not stop me from seeing the natural world. It is as best as I can explain it.

It is a two-level house, there is a dad sitting on the couch reading his newspaper with his legs crossed. He sees his little daughter of about four coming down the stairs. She carries her stuffed animal in her arms, she is without shoes, with her little pajamas that already reached the middle of her leg because she has grown. She is disheveled, with knots in her hair and still with her dirty and tired eyes. The girl approaches her dad and he understands the message... he puts the newspaper off to the side, reaches out to lift her up and places her on his lap.

"My girl came to see me," was his thought. A satisfied smile appeared on her father's face. The girl, without saying a word, rests her head on his chest and closes her eyes. Dad starts stroking her beautiful morning hair and looks at her smiling.

> "I only have *to run* to His arms and let him know that I don't want to start the day without inclining my head on His chest."

At that moment, the voice of God began to speak to my heart and said to me: "Do you think a dad expects something more? Do you think this dad is waiting to have a deep conversation with his daughter? Do you think it is necessary? That carnal and loving father knows that his girl is tired, but that with great sacrifice she rose to be in his arms. She wanted to come to hug him and that has been this little daughter's greatest show of love. There is a smile on that father's face, and his day is full because his girl left her comfort to come to him. Because his little girl put her time with her dad above her sleep time. This girl feels more comfortable on the father's chest than in any other corner of her room. The gesture of that girl filled that father's heart with joy, and nothing has more value for him than that moment.

The image that God showed me this morning made me understand his Paternal heart. God loves me just because. He wants to have a relationship with me as a father wants with his daughter. I do not have to pretend to be, I do not have to say long sentences when I just feel close. I do not have to do a Bible study every morning in fear of being disqualified. I just must run into his arms and let him know that I do not want the day to start without lying on his chest.

I fell asleep in that same corner and woke up knowing that I had slept in his loving arms.

My life is so different now. A beautiful awakening has occurred, and I do not want it to ever stop. One year after my trip to Aruba and my divorce, are about to be completed, I still remember the pain and fear that was in my heart. Today I enjoy mornings of love with Jesus, a full life with my family and friends, and at last, the possibility of beginning to present to my boss some ideas for the summer collection for the following year is outlined. I studied fashion design and it has been extremely difficult to position myself. The competition is very tough, and I do not have the time to go to evening events where other renowned designers go. I do not have the influences or the lifestyle that allows me to move forward. But I know that I will get there. I will become what God wants me to be.

-Epa, mija, (hey daughter) we are coming for you. - It is the voice of Luis picking us up.

-It is getting cold, Luis, - I replied - Are you sure it is a good day to go out on the water? - I asked. I do not have much resistance to cold, but I do for heat.

-I assure you, my girl, you will not regret it. It is a place northwest of where we are, about two hours away. It is a beautiful river full of towering trees on its banks and the reflection on the water is like a dream. While you are in the water, it gives you the impression of jumping from tree to tree.

-Oh, that sounds beautiful. You already convinced me, Luis. "But dress warm," Sandra told me, "it is quite windy, and the temperature does not reach 60° Fahrenheit. Your daughter is coming with us, right?

-Yes, Penelope Sofia has been ready since last night; She cannot wait.

While we were on the road with our boards, ready for adventure, Luis used the time to make a call on speaker phone to his dad in Venezuela. I enjoyed listening to Don Rafael, Luis's father, advising and asking about his brother Raúl, discussing everyday issues and situations of his children and grandchildren. Hearing this tender gentleman express his love for his children was special to me. The fatherhood of a man, his heart for his children and for his grandchildren was special to me because I did not hear it from my own father. And the experience I had this morning began to show me a level of parental love for God that I did not fully know.

As if Luis were listening to my thoughts, he interrupted his subject to ask me: -Daughter, do you know Jehovah's fatherhood?

- I did not know how to respond to that. I did not know if there was a correct answer to that question or if it was a reflection question... For the past six months I had made Jesus my best friend, my beloved, my companion everywhere. But was Jesus my father? I do not think I would know how to respond. I was thoughtful about his question and told him that I was going to think about it and answer it later.

We arrived at the destination and it was a whole new adventure for me because my daughter Penelope Sofia was with us. As I have already told you, I do not know how to swim and if something happens to my little girl I would not think twice about jumping into the water to rescue her, even if it cost me my life. When we arrived at the place, Luis did not lower his regular board, but a box. He approached a group of people who were coordinating the tour and walked away with them. He returned on a gigantic paddleboard. I have never seen a board like that. He said that six people could paddle at the same time on that board.

But it was inflatable, hm! That did not give me much confidence... Until I touched it and I realized that it was as solid as any other.

Luis told me: - Pamela, for your comfort, I brought this board so that your daughter Penelope can go with us. If you want, you can come on this board or you can stay on yours.

I really wanted to experience that place from my own independence, therefore, with affection I replied that I was going to stay with mine, but that I would closely observe his adventure on the gigantic board with my daughter. It gave me confidence knowing that my daughter was in a limo.

"When we believed that we were alone, we were actually resting on the board of salvation, which is His hands."

Sandra, like me, used her personal board, and Luis and Penelope Sofía embarked on the giant one. They were ahead of us. Seeing my daughter sitting comfortably and safely, with Luis directing, gave me the confidence to know that everything would be fine. I knew my daughter was in good hands. He knew that nothing was going to happen to her and that if an incident happened, he would know how to protect her with his own life. It gave me so much peace to know that my daughter was in good hands ...

Suddenly I saw it. I could see that gigantic paddleboard as the enormous hand of God. I could see myself as my little Penelope, covered by the hand of that great Creator. I could see Jesus like Luis, directing the boat, directing destiny, the course of my life. I had a vision of God's care for me. This is my life, this is how God takes care of me, like Luis on the board takes care of Penelope Sofia. He provided the guidance for her on her adventure and provided a much larger board than she might need, just to allow her to feel safe. Tears ran down my cheeks when I thought that in the same way, God the Father cares for us. I understood that if I, in my sinful humanity, was able to give my life for my daughter, how much more God would. I understood the love of the Father. His sacrifice. When mentioned in John 3:16 now makes greater sense to me:

"For this is how God loved the world:
He gave his one and only Son, so
that everyone who believes in him will
not perish but have eternal life."

Today I was able to see, understand God's love and care for widows and orphans. "Father to the fatherless, defender of widows, this is God, whose dwelling is holy." says Psalms 68: 5.

- That is me and my mom. He defends and cares for Mommy, so she has never looked for anyone; He is my Father and he has never left me. Perhaps I did not see Him, I did not understand His presence, but He was there. Always with us. Through Coco, through Penélope and today through Luis, He shows us that he continues to take care of us. My mom and I occupy a preeminent place in the heart of the Father, there is no doubt.

I was crying as I watched that board move with my daughter smiling, confident, simple. And I could see that this is how God saw me. He put my mom's life and mine on His board and protected her during all these years. When we believed that we were alone we were resting on a board of salvation that was His hands. God took us to a safe place, He never allowed us to fall into a dangerous place, I am not helpless, I have Him, my Father loves me and has been with me all my life. I was looking at the landscape. Those tall trees seemed to touch the sky. Some had fallen into the water due to thunderstorms and hurricanes. Even fallen they showed their splendor ...

"Upon receiving the water that gives *life* you will revive and produce everlasting fruits."

-The book of Job says, Pamela, that if the tree is cut down, there is still hope for it; It will still sprout, and its shoots will not be lacking. If its root should grow old in the earth, and its trunk should be dead in the dust, when it perceives the water it will grow green, and it will make a crown like a new plant. That verse should remind you of two things: that you are the hope that your father left on earth, his offspring that today begins to flourish. And that it does not matter that you have fallen, when you receive the life-giving water you will grow green and produce eternal fruits.

- Sandra, Sandra, woman of few words, but when she speaks, the earth trembles. How deep is this woman! I will never be able to see a fallen tree the same way.

-You decide if you go over or under the tree. But you will go to the other side. - She yelled at me as she squatted to go under the tree.

Whoa! what a challenge. We all had to make that decision, and everyone was detained waiting to see how each one was doing it. Some adventurers jumped on the tree and fell on their board on the other side. Luis cautiously and making use of the great balance that he has, he remained standing and promptly crossed his legs over the tree, and being already on the other side he turned and took my daughter by his side and like a leaf he passed her to the other side. We all applauded at the impressive display of control in his movements.

> "As long as you are on your knees in life you will *not fall.*"

A great decision lay in front of me. I decided to apply what I learned: If you are on your knees in life, you will not fall. I got down on my knees, bent my torso and humbled myself, and surrendered. I passed the test on my knees because it is how I prefer to live, in total surrender to His will. The smiles of my daughter, Luis and Sandra confirmed to me that it was the right thing to do.

On the other side of the big fallen tree, we decided to take a short break, and some jumped into the water. It was the perfect excuse to be able to make a change to the plan. I desperately wanted to participate in the experience of sitting on the giant board. So, without any shyness, I asked Luis if I could join him on his board. Sandra was also inspired, and Luis gave us a walk around that beautiful place. Penelope and I lay down on the board while Sandra and Luis paddled. We looked together at the beautiful sky that covered us. That experience! I hugged my little girl and we enjoyed the sun that tenderly reached us.

"This board is His hand that sustains us, the breeze is His love that caresses us, and the sun is His eyes that never stop seeing us."

I enjoyed the sway and movement knowing that I could completely trust these experts that God had put in my way. I enjoyed every minute in that place, letting my Father's love accompany me. This board is His hand that supports me, the breeze is His love that caresses us, the sun is His eyes that do not stop seeing us ...

The Father loves us so much that there is nothing He would not do for us. I knew for the first time what it is to live protected. Calm down. Serene. Resting in the arms of His love. Today I met the love of the Father.

-Luis, I already have an answer to your question. Today I met the love of the Father. It is not something you can study, you feel it. Today I have felt it.

I will go to the
HOUSE
of my
Father.

Walk with the Spirit, enter the mansion

"He lifted me out of the pit of despair, out of the mud and the mire. He set my feet on solid ground and steadied me as I walked along."

PSALMS 40:2

It was my birthday. Almost two years have passed since I met Sandra and Luis, and they decided to give me a nice surprise. They took me to a place called Mount Dora in central Florida. We went paddle boarding on a small river that ran through the city revealing its beautiful nature, on one side trees, parks, and impressive flora, and on the other side cute little houses for people over 55 years old. The river flowed into a large and beautiful natural lake that looked like the ocean. I was prepared with music to enjoy this trip and make this birthday a wonderful one. But God had a different experience in store for me. An even more wonderful one. Before going out into the water, Luis asked me to allow him to pray for me.

- Pamela, today is a special day for you because you are turning 30 years old. It is an important date in your life, and it is the beginning of a new decade. I want to pray that you can receive the best of the gifts that the children of God can have. And it is the gift of his Holy Spirit. Without Him it is difficult to survive the tumultuous conditions of the contaminated water in which we live. It is challenging to cross the high mountains of difficulties. And it is almost impossible to overcome the tides of life. But when we have the Holy Spirit, He guides us to delightful places. He brings peace during any difficult situation. He reveals to our hearts the wishes of the Father. He is our counselor, our helper, and our comforter. And if there is a gift that I would like to ask the Father for you on this day, it is that you can receive his Holy Spirit. - He continued saying: - I have been getting to know you in this year and a half that we have shared, and I have seen the great growth in you. I remember when your mother told you to stay alone for a year and look at you. Now you say it has been two. I want to pray. - And this was his prayer:

Jesus, I cry out to you. Father, I come to you in the name of Jesus, your beloved Son,

*to ask you to baptize your daughter with
the power of your Holy Spirit this morning,
and that this be your gift for this day in
her life. In the name of Jesus, amen.*

His prayer was so simple that I did not really know what to expect. I thought I was going to say a prayer that was going to cause the waters to separate, fireworks to come out of the trees, or the place to shake. But nothing happened. He went very calmly to put his board in the water and told me: "That's it, God did it." I do not know what he saw, but I started to feel cold. I didn't know if it was the nerves of anticipation, I didn't know if it was the product of that prayer, if it was cold or if it was some manifestation of his Holy Spirit in me, but I was trembling. That morning something changed. So subtle, so sublime, so serene, but so deep and so pure that my tears kept running down my cheeks. I did not know if I could ride the board. I felt like trembling and was embarrassed to comment on it, but a knowing look from Sandra changed everything. She approached me gently, put her hand on my shoulder and said to me:
- Calm down, that is the presence of His Holy Spirit. I can only say: Enjoy it! - It was magical, it was supernatural. And I felt so and so not worthy of feeling that beautiful feeling.

I dried my tears trying to overcome myself to start the adventure, but they never stopped coming down. We went on our adventure down the river, but what I was experiencing inside overshadowed all the beauty of that place. Something was still moving inside me, and I was not able to be 100% present enjoying the nature. Once again, the visions began as if God was lowering down a cinema screen to project a film in front of my eyes. It was literally like watching a movie. It was weird because it did not stop me from seeing the river. My natural eyes could see, and I could continue to move on my board safely, without making mistakes. But at the same time, I was seeing something that I could describe as a spiritual vision. I will try to be as detailed as possible by sharing what my eyes saw.

I saw a huge, beautiful mansion. A mansion perhaps like that of some rich famous Hollywood actor. It had an entrance with double oak doors and stained-glass windows. The doors were tall, perhaps three times taller than me. I went to that door and wanted to knock, but I did not; I just stopped. My dress was torn, my hair was messy, I had knots in my hair, my suit was full of mud, I was barefoot. I had bruises on my body, tears, blood was leaking from somewhere in my stomach, or in my heart. It was me, but very battered.

The door opened without touching it. As if they had been waiting for me. At the door, a kind gentleman received me. Behind him three or four beautiful maidens dressed as elegant servants. I use the word maidens because I do not know how else to describe them. They were so pretty, so sweet, their clothes were beautiful, clean, smiling, mature, subtle, ready with a smile to serve. The knight was noble and very correct. They invited me in and took me by the hand. From the moment I walked through the door, the maids began to comb my hair, take rubbish off me, and attend to me.

I walked a few steps and in front of me was Jesus. Radiant, smiling, confident, King. It had to be Him. I cannot describe his physical appearance in detail, but his presence was unique. It was peace. I had this feeling of standing in front of someone so big, so pure, so mine and I so his, but so Holy. He hugged me like a girl, held my face and said: - You are home, daughter. All old things happened; I will make all new ones. You are in the right place and here I will take care of you. I will heal each of your wounds, I will heal each of your sores, I will cover you with my blood, I will cleanse you with my love, I will remove the scales from your eyes, I will brush your hair and I will make you see my will for your life. I have brought you here to take care of you. -

He walked with me and began to show me the palace where I was going to be living, and he said to me: - This is the place where my

> "I will heal every one of your wounds, I will mend each of your sores, I will cover you with my blood, I will clean you with my love, I will remove the scales of your eyes, I will brush your hair and I will make you see *my will* for your life."

children live and you are one of them. But there is a special place where my children spend a season to be healed. I suddenly interrupted him, and crying out, I asked him: "Please, Lord, do not put me away from you, where I only want to be is at your feet, I can live there. Do not send me anywhere far from you. Let me live at your feet. Let me dwell in the place of your presence. I want to walk with you, and I want to make sure I do not get away from there. Let me live at your feet, tie me to them and do not let me go. He looked at me and smiled softly, hugged me, and gave me peace."

> "Let me *live* at Your feet. Let me dwell in the place of Your presence."

He walked with me to a small room on the first level of the great mansion. I could see stairs to a wide place, and I saw people living and coexisting in that beautiful place. They were smiling, talking, everyone was shiny, beautiful people, and full of a special joy that I did not have. He looked at me, and he looked at them and observing the people he said to me: - Easy, daughter, one day very soon you will be there with your brothers. But for now, I want you in this special place. -

He took me to this little room. It had a single bed, a small table, and a lamp. Everything was white and pink. From the small room I could see a great throne. I could not see the whole of that throne; I saw only one of the legs of the throne, golden as the sun. I knew it was the throne of God, so it would be at his feet. At this point I thought: "either I am crazy, or I have a caricature vision." But I did not want the vision to stop at all.

I could see a gigantic foot and I knew it was my heavenly Father's. Jesus said to me: - The desire of your heart will be fulfilled. You will live at the feet of the Master. No one will take you away. No one will be able to take you by force and take you out of my will because to go against you, they would have to intervene with me. You will live at my feet and here you will be healed. - I noticed that in the small room there was a scenic window.

I looked at it curiously without comment, but He did not let me guess. - I have left that window so that you know that you are free to leave. If at some point you decide to go out and not live in this place anymore, you can do it. The window is open; you can leave at any time. You need to know that this window is the entrance to the outside world, therefore, temptations and the past will come to stand at it to invite you out. I am not going to close it because you should be the one to freely decide. I do not force anyone. It will be your will. Many times, you have been here, I have brought you to this place and you have escaped into your past towards the temptations of this world, towards the muddy muck. You have fallen into the hands of many criminals who have left you as you are today. The marks you have today are the result of the times you have escaped through that window to return to your past or to go after the temptations of this world. Each time you have hit yourself hard, you have hurt your knees, it has destroyed your clothes, you have muddied your face. You have been attacked by ferocious lions and predatory wolves. All the abuse you have experienced can be left behind if you stay in this safe room. It is up to you. If at any time you want to close that window forever, it is you who must do it. I will never abandon you or leave you, but neither will I force you to stay. –

I felt so welcomed in that beautiful place that I could not understand how I could be tempted to get out of it. But I recognized that I had done it many times before. The vision continued and I could see how people from my past stood at that window to invite me out for a walk. I could see that that window was many times the social networks that tempted me to go looking for what God did not send me to look for.

I want someone God-given and not someone I seek myself. I do not want to go back to the past, but to walk towards the future. But I could clearly see each of the people and situations that stood in that window to talk to me, particularly during the nights, when I tried to sleep and my thoughts woke me up giving me great ideas of how I could solve my life myself if I did such things, or if I invited this or that person to look for me in my room. Years passed in my vision and I could see how my appearance was improving every day, how my hair began to soften, how the wounds began to heal. My dresses were different; these were white and clean and ironed.

We reached the end of our trip in the river and it was time to rest and return. I did not want to interrupt what I was experiencing and as if they had perceived it, Luis said to me:

-Pamela, do you want us to turn around or continue paddling? I see that you are silent, and I imagine that you are in the presence of God.

—So much wisdom God has given in his years of walking with Him. - Yes, Luis, I want to continue, I do not want to talk now.

The vision returned. I had beautiful slippers so comfortable and shiny. I felt like a princess. I could see myself every day getting up in the peace of Christ. I was walking and my breakfast was served. I shared the table with Jesus, his Holy Spirit guided me to the gardens, and I enjoyed the flowers and the little birds. I ran through his gardens like a little girl, and every day my heart healed a little more. I could see the transformation happening in my physical appearance, as a reflection of what was happening to my soul. The happy heart beautifies the face, there is no doubt about it.

A few minutes passed and the vision stopped. I meditated on it and my heart leaped with emotion. This is where I am. I promised my mom a year not to look at anyone. I think I can go for a few more. I do not want to be wrong again. I decided to give myself up to the process and heal. I decided to wait and trust that if it is God's will, He will bring me the right person at the right time.

I was captivated by the vision in the Spirit that I had received. If this is walking in the Spirit, I want this every day of my life. His Holy Spirit had allowed me to see where I was spiritually. He let me see how I got there, what process I am in and where I am going. How my confidence grew when I learned that I live in the King's palace! That my room is at his feet, that my daily company is his Spirit. Know that He has assigned angels to take care of me. I am not worthy of so much. Never in my life have I experienced so much care for myself. I do not know what the life of rich people is. I do not know what it is like to be served by someone else. I do not know what it feels like for someone to serve your food, clean your house and make your bed. Much less can I imagine that someone brushes my hair, changes my clothes and cares for me with so much love. This level of love surpasses me. It breaks in me all feelings of orphanhood and abandonment. It shows me a level of love and compassion from the Father that I never thought I knew.

> "There's a *place* reserved for the afflicted in the heart, for the broken, for the lonely, for the stained, for the mistreated."

This vision is mine and I share it knowing that some will say that it has no theological basis or that it is not Biblical. Honestly, what the world thinks I do not care. What this vision produced in my spirit was a total infatuation with his Holy Spirit. The fruit that this vision gave in my life changed my way of seeing the love of God. It was what I needed, and I believe with all my heart that God gave it to me because I needed to believe that He cares for me. I needed to believe that there is a future and a hope. I needed to know that there is a place reserved for the heartbroken, for the broken, for the lonely, for the muddy, for the abused. I needed to know that there is a personal place where God cares for us. I also needed to know that at some point I will be healthy, free, and happy with other brothers and sisters of the faith. But right now, I just want to be at his feet.

Upon returning to the shore I was still weeping and silent as when we left. But my face was not that of anguish, but that of peace, a face that showed the fullness of Christ. Luis looked at me smiling and said: - I do not know what has happened inside you, but I know that God has allowed you to have the best birthday gift of your life until today. And you can be sure that what He has promised you He will do, and what He has shown you will come true. You are in the arms of the Lord and He cares for you. I answered correcting him: -No, I know where I am, and I am at the feet of Christ, the best place where I can be, the safest.

> "His feet are my place of *rest*, my dwelling."

blog

There is no greater beauty in nature than that found in the supernatural arms of God. The vision that God has for your life, with your human eyes you cannot see it. I want to walk in the Spirit every day, knowing that I live in heavenly places. His Holy Spirit will take me to unsuspected places and will make me live inexplicable experiences.

I have fallen in love with his Holy Spirit and I do not want to live anywhere other than in the place of His presence. I want to live at His feet His and know that I am at His fingertips. That His feet are the place of my rest, my room. I do not want to go back; I do not want temptation and the past to drag me to a window of pain. I decide to look towards the throne of his grace, I decide to look towards the light of His presence. I decide to walk in the gardens of His love, I decide to smile at the touch of His Spirit and at His voice run to go to dinner with Jesus. Every day I want to live in the palaces of His love.

If this message has touched your heart, share it, and bless others on social media using #Myboardofsalvation

 SHARE

Chapter
17

The *crown*

"Blessed is a man who perseveres under trial; for once he has been approved, he will receive the crown of life which the Lord has promised to those who love Him."

JAMES 1:12 (NASB)

I love you, Lord, I never want to get away from your presence. I need your love, I need your presence, I need to know you more, fill myself more. In my strength, my Lord, I constantly fail. But I believe that in you, I will find the way, in your arms I feel full of joy. In your presence I feel complete. It is for your love that I have been able to overcome so many things, and if I am standing today it is because you have supported me. Your arm lifted me up and has never left me. I love you Lord.".

That was my prayer this morning. I have understood that God's purpose for me this season cannot be accomplished if it is not in constant prayer. It is the only thing that keeps me focused. But night falls and the war rages. It is so difficult when night comes, and I put Penelope to bed. After working several hours on schoolwork, I wish I could go to my room and have someone to share my adult conversations with. I slept with my mom in bed since I was five years old, then Sofia came, and we all three slept together until she was 5.

After my divorce, my daughter and I slept together until just a few months ago when I started sleeping alone.

It feels so weird to get to my room and be alone. We are three women in this house. - Lord, have mercy on us, bring a man to take care of us. - That is my prayer always. I think it has a hint of attempted manipulation, but it is subtle. But I have already understood that it is a lost case. Trying to manipulate God does not work, and maybe it even slows me down. But it feels like a desert in my chest, a cold of loneliness. When night comes, I just want to cry and try one more time to convince him to change the plan. And He reminds me of that window. That window allows me to leave if I wish, that allows me to re-select on my own. That window also represents falls, stumbles, bad decisions, and pain. I cannot deny that at times I think about taking a risk and go out of the window once more. In short, God's mercies are new every morning, says his Word. If I make a small mistake, perhaps the same He will forgive me. All these thoughts cross my mind and that is when I open my computer and access my Blog, my board of salvation, and start writing to relax a little.

Suddenly the thought: "What if my ex has changed? Perhaps he reflected and misses me and wants to return, to be Sofia's father and take care of us. People change. I've changed". And in the middle of my private mental conversation with myself, God in his love and wisdom interrupts me saying:

- My daughter, just wait a little longer, do not do it today, wait for tomorrow. - His sweet answer melts my heart. - Not today, come today, lie on my chest and rest on me and you will see that tomorrow will be a better day. Daughter, just for today, do not look back. Today you are tired, and you must rest. His sweet words, like a father, comfort my soul and give me hope. In his arms I fall asleep crying, feeling lonely, but knowing that I am loved.

I got up charged with energy to start the day and went to the meeting point. This time we are going with a large group. Luis told me that there are 30 people registered on the tour to go out to do paddle boarding. Sandra and Luis will be the ones to lead the group, and I am one of the 30 people who will follow them through the trip. Every experience is exciting; I always learn something; I always have a new experience.

We met for an orientation from Luis of what we should be doing, the challenges we would face and some techniques. Everyone who came to this tour must already have previous experience. But this time he did something different: He asked each of the attendees, many of them his private students, to tell the biggest challenge they had faced while doing paddle board, and how they had solved it. Each one got up and told different experiences, all interesting, many very funny, and others a little intimidating. I had no idea what I was going to share. When it was my turn, I realized that I was the last to share. I got up like the others and began to say the only thing that was in my heart and that God had shown me while I waited. I did not know how it was going to be taken. I had never openly shared my faith before a group of people, or person to person either. My relationship with God was completely private and I was not comfortable sharing or speaking about it; I could do it easier in writing. But anyway, I stopped, and this is what I said:

-I must confess that the biggest challenge I experienced doing paddle board was in my first experience. I was in Aruba and it was where I met Luis. It happened that without realizing it I went away and ended up in the open sea, where boats and all kinds of jet skis passed. I don't know how to swim and the only thing that came to my mind was to follow an instruction Luis gave me: - If the situation becomes difficult, get down on your knees and sink deep the oar so you can advance in the direction you want. - But the address Luis gave me, I must confess, was accompanied by a subtle voice in my heart that began to give me specific indications of what I was doing. It was the voice of God saying to me: "When things are going to get tough, the best place you can be is on your knees. That is always the safest place; if you fall it should be on your knees. Your knees guarantee you not to fall into the depth of the sea". That voice went on to tell me: "Once you are on your knees, go deep with me, go deep into my scriptures, burst thirsty into the depth of my presence and you will see how you will advance to go out to a safe place in your life. Depth will help you move in the direction you want. "- Those words marked my destiny. Since then, the voice of God has guided me in every challenge in my life. And I want to invite you that if you are going to give yourself the opportunity to go out into the waters to try to walk on the sea on a board, do not waste time with nonsense; talk to God. He manifests himself in different ways to our lives and I guarantee that if you listen to his voice and do what he tells you, everything in your life will be fine.

-I am a testimony that in each of my experiences on that board the Lord has spoken to me. And I am a living testimony that God has turned my life around in a way that I never expected to experience before Him. Luis is a witness. I walk with God holding hands and go on my knees to fight each of my battles. I invade the depth of his presence to find refuge and to advance. -At that point, my throat was dry, and I started to cough, my lips were so dry that I could barely move them. I did not know what was happening to my body, but a tremor would not let me continue. It was the second time that I felt a tremor like that and felt vulnerable. I was unable to resist the fear I had in my heart for what I had just done. I had never exposed my heart like that. I felt embarrassed and exposed.

I looked at Luis for help, and his smile on his face was followed by the eruption of applause. He stood up and everyone followed him. I never expected a reaction like that. Without realizing it, I witnessed to them my faith. The Holy Spirit came upon me and took control of my words. I liked that; I did not anticipate that moment. It was a very emotional moment. I felt privileged.

> "Going deep helps you *go* in the direction you want."

We went into the water with our boards and I started paddling, but my heart was startled. I was so excited that I could not stop crying. And suddenly once again I began to have one of those experiences that I cannot tell you if they happen here on earth, or God took me to heaven. But this was more than a screen vision; it felt three-dimensional. I was experiencing a different and coexistent reality from the one I was living physically.

I was advancing on my board when suddenly I began to feel as if the sky was beginning to open. A "sunroof" effect is how I can best describe it. I started looking at another sky, and in that other sky there was a celebration. I could see people's feet jumping and dancing. There was something like confetti, a great celebration. Suddenly they began to give me entrance to this party and I could not say how, but I began to have the feeling of moving upwards, towards that sky. I was physically on my board in the water, but at the same time I felt in that place. I felt the hugs of each one of the people who were there in that place welcoming me. Congratulating me and wishing me the best in this walk.

I cannot explain it in better words, but it was a celebration and I was invited. I did not quite understand what it was about. Suddenly I was walking like on a catwalk. I stopped and saw a lot of excited people. Someone put a seal on me, another person came over me and gave me flowers, and a third person approached me and placed a crown on my head. I was crowned. I did not understand anything. I was still standing on my board, but the feeling of realism was so great that I had to touch my head to confirm. So real was the feeling that someone had placed a crown on me that I was afraid it would fall off as I continued. I was trying to balance and move delicately; I did not want to do anything to make my crown fall into the water.

I felt at that time like Miss Universe, excuse me for being too cheesy or lack of humility; I reveal to you my most intimate feeling of that day. I cannot explain any other way and my vision may sound ridiculous. But I promise you, that is how I lived it. What I felt at the time was that I was welcomed into a kingdom and in this kingdom, everyone had crowns. That the Lord selected me and officially made me his princess. That in front of His entire kingdom He presented me as a princess, His daughter. And they all celebrated me by welcoming me to this beautiful new place. That was the most dramatic and exhilarating paddle board experience of my life. The whole time I stood up straight, like a princess taking care of her crown. I did not know if people saw or did not see my crown, but I was sure that there was one on my head, so much so that I approached Sandra and asked: - Sandra, do you see anything on my head? She looked at me strangely, pointed her eyes at my head and said: -No, my beautiful princess, I do not see anything on your head. You are perfect. - She does not know that with her words, when she called me princess, she gave me more hope; confirming what had just happened.

"Blessed is a man who perseveres under trial; for once he has been approved, he will receive the crown of life which the Lord has promised to those who love Him." James 1:12 (NASB)

blog The times of desert and loneliness are those moments that God uses most to show us his plans for our lives and the way He looks at us.

- I learned that if when you are waiting you think about going back, you just must stop, rest in his arms, and wait a little longer. The temptation will pass if you do not act on it.
- I understood that I do not need to do an act of great execution before the presence of God every day. Just coming into his arms is enough to express that I love him.
- I discovered the power of our testimony. When the Holy Spirit speaks through us in time and out of time, great things happen. We are not ashamed of the gospel because it is the power of God.
- I received the crown of life. Without knowing it, I passed a test and received the crown of life. Today I know that I am part of a new kingdom.

If this has touched your heart and your life, I invite you to pray with me so that his Holy Spirit shows you the depths of his love and that He does great things in you. Share this message on your social networks and use #Myboardofsalvation - Let us stay connected.

 SHARE

Chapter
18

Prophetic
arm

"He has done mighty deeds with His arm;
He has scattered those who were proud
in the thoughts of their heart."

LUKE 1:51

I have thoroughly enjoyed this journey. Today Pamela is nothing like what she was. It is about to be 5 years since this adventure began in Aruba and I have been able to mature deeply in the love of Christ. I look with great sadness at suicide rates, and I want to blog about it because I am ready to do it.

blog

I must confess that thoughts of suicide were something that had been accompanying me since childhood. I cannot remember when they started, but I think it was close to the date Coco died. The idea of looking for a way to cease to exist on this earthly plane and go to heaven crossed my mind seriously, according to what I understood was going to happen within my humble description as a child. I remember I took a piece of these yellow notebooks that everyone has in their house and started writing a letter to God. In that letter I asked him to please accept me in heaven, to receive me, because somehow, I was going to end my life.

I began to analyze that the blue pills which kill mice could be highly effective for my passage to heaven. In my letter I said to the Lord that I did not know him, but that I had heard Coco mention it when he went to heaven; that he would also receive me. When I finished writing these sincere lines, I began to feel a voice inside me that spoke to me with great affection and told me things that brought me peace. That voice became so strong inside me, and without much thought I began to write what that voice told me. And those words were:

-Daughter, you will not die, but you will live to tell your testimony. Because from this day on, I will be your father and you will be my daughter. Do not fear because this slight tribulation will pass. I will take care of you every day of my life, as a father does with his daughter. I will take you to places you cannot imagine, and you will help the orphan and the lonely, the abandoned and the widow, and the needy and the broken. –

When I finished writing the words that flowed from my heart, I felt so much peace that I fell asleep hugging that paper. This experience marked my life. I knew that although I did not understand everything, there was a superior being who had the ability to speak to me and I could hear him, and he had the ability to take care of me in situations that I did not know. But that experience did not stop there, it was only the first.

There was another one that marked me on a much deeper level. The letter. A letter of 6 pages that I keep with a very deep value. I took it to Aruba and read it almost daily.

It was the day I decided to buy my ticket to Aruba, almost 5 years ago. I had been driving from my job and I had a great affliction, a strong pain in my heart. Once again, my relationship had ended in failure. Once again, I made a mistake, once again I modeled a bad example for my daughter. What am I going to do with my life? I asked myself anguished.

-Pamela, you constantly make wrong decisions, you are wrong in everything you do and truly if your mother was able to raise you alone without the help of anyone, she will also surely be able to do a better job with your daughter, Penelope Sofia. Why don't you get out of the way? Why don't you take your life? Do not be a hindrance to your daughter, she will be better in the hands of your mother. It is better that she has a good memory of who you were, instead of shaming her every day of her life. -

-These were the thoughts running through my mind. Anguish seized me because as I listened to them, I received them as mine. Today I know that voice was that of the enemy, but I did not know it that day.

-Every thought pushed me deeper into the abyss, but suddenly that other voice, that other voice that I had heard, came back to me. That voice that would become my board of salvation. That voice would rescue me. And that voice spoke to me with a strong voice this time, and it said to me:

- Enough, enough, enough, my daughter. Can't you see how much I have taken care of you? Don't you realize that I gave my life for you? Have you not noticed that I have taken care of you night and day; What do I take care of: your daughter, your mother, and your family? Don't you realize that if you are here, it is on me? –

-It was funny because this voice not only spoke to me regularly. That voice resounded like a symphony. In a way I cannot describe, His voice sounded like a rhyme. The prayers among each other rhymed. And nothing I heard from inside came, that is, it was not the product of my mind. I did not think the way this voice spoke to me. I was not able to rhyme as this voice did. Each phrase was a symphony.

-I could not wait to get home. I had an urge to go write everything this voice told me. I drove harder than ever to get home, open my computer, and started taking dictation. That was what I felt. I began to write to the dictation of the voice each word that came from inside me. I filled six pages of a deep intimate conversation between my Heavenly Father and myself. I had never had an experience like that. He proclaimed saying: - Stop your bad thoughts, pause your bad way, put your gaze on me. –

-It was a cry from a Father in pain; I felt that with a strong voice He said to me: - Do what you have to do, my daughter, but for a moment stop your life. -He told me, but lovingly reminded me of how much He had done for me. The most incredible thing was that I had never read the Bible in my life, and Biblical verses that I did not know began to flow and I wrote. This did not come from me, it was impossible. This came from

God. Six pages marked my life. Six pages drew me to
Him, to the Messiah. He told me so much, he told me
everything. He told me of my gifts and my purpose.
He spoke to me of the prophetic, which I did not
understand. He told me about promises hidden in the
Bible. He spoke to me of a future and a hope, he spoke
to me of a second coming. He spoke to me of his Son
and his sacrifice, and he spoke to me of his love poured
out on a cross for me.

-He made me promise to close the door to take
my life. He made me understand that He had a plan
and that it was time to move from the driver's seat
to the passenger's seat. That it was time to give him
the keys to my life. It was time to rest and wait in
the power of his salvation and redemption. I ended
up exhausted from writing that letter. There were
six pages dictated by God that marked my life until
today.

- It was so much, and it meant so much that when I
finished it, I decided that I needed some time to reflect
on what had happened. I needed to understand and
know that it was God who spoke to me. I took the letter
to my psychologist Lisa. She was also an associate
pastor in the church she attended and knew the Word
well. When she read it, she cried and said to me:

- There is no doubt that this letter was dictated
by God. I know that you do not know what you have
written. And I know that our Father's love letters are

love poems and often rhyme. Beloved, you need time to process everything that it says here. Why don't you take a few days and go to meditate alone? How about Aruba? Have you been there? It is quiet, beautiful, and full of nature. It could be any other place, that was the first one that came to my mind. Take some time to meditate on what God is talking about in your life because there is something else here. There is a purpose to writing.

-Her words were confirmation of what I had felt, and at that moment and without a doubt I arrived at my house, got the ticket, and decided to go to Aruba.

If this topic touches your heart and you want to save a life, share it on your networks and use #Myboardofsalvation and #yourlifeispriceless #NOtosuicide

All glory be to God, Lord of my life.

 SHARE

I confess that telling this testimony on my blog today is an exercise in stretching and humility. Acknowledging my past thoughts of suicide is not something I do every day. I look back and hold

myself accountable for having those thoughts in my mind, for considering abandoning my mom when she needed me most, and for considering abandoning my poor daughter who is not to blame for any of this. But I have felt that sharing it has a purpose. If it can save someone else's life, it has been worth it.

I have at this moment a desire, a phrase inside me that flutters in me indescribably. I feel that I need to write ... No, I must rephrase, I hear His strong voice inside me saying: - My daughter, if you are not ashamed of me and my power, give me the glory. God knows I struggle with saying phrases or writing phrases that sound like what I call "Christianese". And that is perhaps one of them. I struggled inside for a moment with what I am feeling, but without being able to contain myself, I closed my blog saying:

All glory be to God, Lord of my life.

As I wrote that phrase a warmth came over me and an indescribable presence embraced me. I do not know how much that meant to my Lord, but I get the impression that something was broken. Something broke inside me and something broke in the sky; something broke. The presence that is upon me at this moment I cannot describe. Tears run down my cheeks because I feel that today's blog did something special in heaven and I cannot understand it, but I can feel it. I think it is the beginning of something. I have the anticipation that something will happen.

At that moment I looked at the clock and said: "Whoa! Sandra and Luis are waiting for me to go paddle boarding. Today we have a date on the beach, and it is time for me to be at the meeting place. I am an hour away. "I hurry to collect my things to mount up in my soaring blue RAM pickup. People see me and they cannot believe that truck is mine. Sometimes it is difficult to handle the small details of owning a truck. The doors are heavy, tall, and I am of medium height. I had my wallet in hand, my iPad, and my camera on one side, and on the other I had my board. I walked to get it into the back of the truck and the board was obviously too heavy, so I was making a bigger effort to mount it. I typically have help.

I put the board on the ground, opened the back of the truck, and lifted the board to place it on the truck using all my strength to lift it, when indescribably it felt like it was slipping out of my hands. I will try to explain it. Do you know when you do a greater force to lift something very heavy, but when you lift it you realize that it is empty, so it does not weigh anything and you feel like it is flying out of your hand?

Something like that was the feeling that I can describe to you. I raised the board and it became so light that I was surprised. I had to look to know what was happening and the moment I looked I saw an arm that was holding it on the other side; it was a man's arm. I know because he had hair, he was male. I was scared, my heart pounded because the first thing I thought was that someone had come to assault me, that someone was going to attack me. There was a stranger next to me and there was no male in my house. I looked everywhere looking for where the man is on the arm and I did not see anyone, since the board was inside my truck. That arm and I put it inside, but I do not see the owner of that arm.

I went around the same place twice looking for where the arm came from and I did not see it. No one can deny me what my eyes have seen. As I turned around, a 360 ° turn, and realizing that no one was there, I began to feel the presence of the Holy Spirit. I began to feel that something supernatural had just happened. I began to realize that I had a brief visitation. But is it possible that I have seen the arm of God? Is it possible that Jesus was here for a second? Is it possible that his Holy Spirit took the shape of an arm for a moment and made me see that he really is my helper? Is it possible? I am not worthy to receive such an experience. The cry overwhelmed me in such a way that I was not able to sit up. That trembling again took hold of me, I began to speak in tongues that I do not know, and I felt that an indescribable fire ran through my whole body. It is that I am not worthy, I cried, it is that I do not deserve, it is that I am such a little thing, Lord. It is that I do not deserve anything from you, it is that my hands are dirty, my body is dirty, it is that I do not deserve, Lord, I am not worthy. How did you give me a moment like this? Maybe it is hard to believe what I am saying, but I know what I saw, I saw what I saw, I know what I felt, but nobody will understand. They will tell me that I am crazy, that I imagined it. They will tell me what they want, but I know that one day I will go to heaven, I will run hysterical into the arms of my Father, and I have to ask him: "Was that your arm? Tell me, did you let this needy woman see your arm? Tell me, I need to know. No one is going to answer that question; only you, Jesus. One day I will ask you and you would answer me, if I imagined it or if you allowed this humble single mother to have seen your arm".

"With whom My hand will be established; My arm also will strengthen him." Psalm 89:21 (NASB)

"the great trials which your eyes saw and the signs and the wonders and the mighty hand and the outstretched arm by which the Lord your God brought you out. So shall the Lord your God do to all the peoples of whom you are afraid." Deuteronomy 7:19 (NASB)

He came
TO MY
rescue

Chapter
19

Is it the *end* or the *beginning*?

"Only I can tell you the future before it even happens. Everything I plan will come to pass, for I do whatever I wish."

ISAIAH 46:10

Today, it has been five years since that moment when I got on a plane to go to Aruba and a new story in my life began. That moment when the impact of God's presence was so great that I could not be the person I was before. Here I am with my feet propped up on the suitcase, barefoot, my sandals on the airport floor. I love to travel comfortably; I would like to dare to travel in pajamas! I am on my way to a meeting I do not know what to expect. I have my iPad in my lap, and I cannot miss this opportunity to start writing about what I am feeling and what I am going to live with. The Pamela who returns to Aruba is not the same as she was five years ago. That girl did not have a hobby, nor so many friends. Now I live daily with my paddle board and life coaches. Who would have guessed that?

Five years ago, I left my 10-year-old girl at home with my mom. Today I left a young lady of 15 who fills me with pride. And today I return in love. Five years ago, I came to Aruba broken into 1,000 pieces, divorced, ashamed, destroyed and without any hope. I went looking for an escape, a rest, and an explanation. I came with a 6-page letter full of illusion. This time I return because I have seen the arm of God at work in my life, because I have been crowned with his mercies and because I have fallen deeply in love with his Holy Spirit and His presence in my life.

I feel that on this trip I am not going alone, I come with my friend Jesus. It is like it is our honeymoon. What is more, I will imagine that I am going on a honeymoon with my beloved. That we will spend some spectacular days in Aruba. God has restored my life, changed my wailing dance, and made me a new person. I thought that by this date I would have already found the love of a man, I gave myself a year and five have passed ... And what I found was real love. I have managed to fall in love with God. I feel complete, full, and happy, I feel capable. The life before me fills me with expectations. I am leaving because I want to make a space to meditate and prepare for what is to come. I want to make a covenant with God about the next years of my life.

I am already in the hotel room in the same pictorial place where I stayed five years ago. So many memories come to my mind: a brief air of nostalgia for what I was and what I am no longer. I miss Sandra and Luis because here I met them. I never imagined that on a temporary vacation I would find so many permanent things for myself. Sandra and Luisito are those mentors that I needed in my life. The paddle board has been more than entertainment; It has been an excuse that God has used to speak to my heart clearer than ever. And time has been healing. But above all, what has helped me is his Holy Spirit, my counselor. I cannot wait to get on the board and start my adventure here in Aruba. What could I learn these days? What new experiences will I take? I am ready to live. I am ready to start again.

It is Saturday morning and I have had a wonderful night. I rested and I am more awake than ever, ready to return to the place where it all started. Walking along the beach, I meditated on how many people are here who perhaps are where I was. Is it possible that God has brought me back here so I can go and touch other people's lives, and tell what God has done in my life? Will I be ready to help others? - God, use me, tell me, what should I do? What should I say? At that time, his voice was so real.

As if having a conversation with my best friend, his response came immediately.

- Daughter, there is time for everything and there will be time to talk. I have brought you here to listen. I have brought you here to give you what you still lack. You have accomplished so much; you have come a long way. But fear is undoubtedly an impediment to growth.

-Fear? But I have been braving enough to get to this place alone, I have taken a plane and I have ventured to do so many things. I have always felt safe and brave.

- Why do you fear being abandoned, daughter? Why do you continue to fear rejection? Why do you limit yourself in your expectations? Why are you afraid to hope for the best?

Each of these questions was like a dagger to my heart. But it was a different pain. It was a pain similar to what you feel when a sharp object is going to be removed from your body, and it is necessary to cut the skin a little so that the piece of glass comes out and vacates a place that does not belong to it. It was that impact pain that caused the blood to gush out, but you know relief is near.

I had to sit down on the sand, where I was walking; I had to catch my breath and hold back my tears, it was impossible. Each of those questions had a root in my heart. There were four questions he asked me, and I had to answer:

- Yes, I am afraid. I am afraid that something good will happen to me and then it will be rejected. I am afraid it will not be enough. I have tried to overcome

1,000 ways, but this inner fear tells me 'there is nothing good for you'. I even confess that I fear having a premature death like my father's, and perhaps that was the reason why suicide continually appeared in my head. I would rather go than be taken out. To what extent I was a slave to fear, I did not know.

I needed to sit a few hours on the sand and was surprised to see that there was still so much work for God to do in me. And I was wondering: Lord, when are you going to finish me? How much more is missing? I felt the voice of the Lord answer me: - You are missing a lot, my daughter, you have a life left. - Followed by that, an instruction. - Dare to face all your fears. -

At that moment, I understood that it was a good time to rent a board and launch myself into the adventure. I did not have to search far. Next to me I saw an American boy in a "Rastafari" style, but with blue eyes and blond hair, tan skin from the sun and his hair in dreads. A unique combination. I saw him come and go delivering surfboards, jet skis and paddle boards. I approached him and asked: "Excuse me, are you the person in charge of renting?" - Yes ma'am, this is me. I am Billy. How can I help you? - I started asking him about the prices and the best places to practice paddle board.

He seems to have perceived that I had previous experience and felt confident to challenge me. - Listen, why don't you go to the west side of the island? We have good waves there and I have a dude that is training people for surfing on a paddle board ...- My eyes widened, and all the fears came to the surface. And at that moment I remembered: "It is time to overcome all my fears." Without much thought I said yes and followed his directions to approach the place he was talking about. The view was spectacular in that place. Some rocks separated the passive beach from the waves that seemed to swell before my eyes. My heart was pounding, but I said to myself, if God is with me, who can be against me? I am going to do it. I approached the coach, I told him about the experience I had, and he told me to enter the water. - I want to see you for a little while and in an hour, when the other group starts, I will train you. –

That gave me peace. I was going to have time to relate to the power of the waves, and in an hour, I could decide whether that was for me. I took my board and decided to jump into the water. It seems that an army was fighting against me. I used all my strength just to lie on the board and it was impossible to keep up. The waves washed over me and sent me back onto the sand. I tried and tried, but the force of the sea overwhelmed me. I started trying to go underneath the waves looking to get to a point where the waves did not break so hard and I could at least be on my board. I knew that if I could at least get on my knees on the board, the waves would not knock me out of there. I tried unsuccessfully. After much trying, I finally made it.

I was on my knees in the water. Here comes a big wave; I am going to stay on my knees, and I will not even try to stand up. I will hold onto the board strong and pass this goal without fear. The wave came, lifted me up, maybe five feet above sea level, the wave passed, and I was able to stay on. As I celebrated the wave that had just passed, the next one was getting even bigger. It crashed on me and dragged me swallowing water and sand back to shore. I started to think, "Well, I think this is not for me. Perhaps I was wrong to think that I heard the voice of God; Maybe all this time I was wrong. Maybe this is all a drama that I believed in my head, and I am not for this. Maybe if I go to the gym, do weights for a while, run and learn to swim..."

I was frustrated, scared, and determined not even to try, when the young man who was training approached me and asked if I was ready. -What if I am ready? I'm ready to go, "I replied. He started to laugh and said to me: - Nothing happened, you are not the first and you are not going to be the last. Confront fear, that is all. His words were like another stab in my heart. But it is that God uses even donkeys, nothing personal against the boy, but how is it possible to tell me the same thing that God was saying in my ear? I got up and said: "Now I am more afraid than at the beginning. So, I have to do it. "

I started to follow him. At least I would not be alone and there were five other crazy people with me. I cannot tell you how wonderful an experience I have had today. What if I fell? Hundreds of times, I lost count. What if I got scared? I thought it would be the last day of my life in each wave. I asked: who comes up with this silly idea? I thought of my daughter and her wisdom and my lack of it; I thought of my mother, her advice. It would not even sound funny to my mother. But despite everything, I had a great day. I do not know if I would try again, but something came out of me. A fear that overcame and stopped me was gone. Knowing that I could do it made me see how strong I am and that no matter how difficult the circumstances become, I would get over it. For the first time I felt a certainty that I would survive. That was new to me. I felt so full. So happy. The sunset in that place was beautiful and I wanted to see it from the water. Nothing new or complicated. I just wanted to lie down on a board and think.

I went over on my board one more time and approached an area that had no waves. It looked passive and had a beautiful view on the east side of the rocks. I started paddling and enjoying every meter of that beautiful sea. I felt so full and so confident that I was not afraid to go deep. It was the first time I had strayed so far from the shore. But I had peace. I saw the vastness of the sea, but so passive. So serene. I compared it to the majesty of God. Large, imposing, sublime, serene, impressive, intimidating, but a presence that makes you fall in love. I might have been a mile or more from shore. Maybe 30 feet deep. Maybe more. But the peace that passes all understanding wrapped me up in such a way that I cannot explain it to myself.

I sat on my board to enjoy the sunset from there. I did not intend to return to the shore at night, but I did want to start watching the sunset from that beautiful place. The sun was going down, and it made me think about how many seasons we have left to spend. Every time the sun goes down, it gives us a new opportunity to reflect. Every day is a great opportunity. I lay down on the board while I reflected and allowed myself to enjoy the orange, yellow, blue, and pink colors of the sky. A light show.

I decided to unzip the "leash" from my ankle, because at the end of the day there were no waves and I was really lying down. I think it was an inopportune mistake on my part. The minutes had passed, and that heavenly peace was such that I did not know if I was in heaven or on earth. I could enjoy every breath; I had so much peace.

Suddenly I felt a small wave, something began to rise ... My board was rising, it seemed to be lying in the air. It did not take long for me to realize that this was not a wave, but an animal. Under my board was passing the largest animal I have ever seen. It was a huge whale. My heart raced, my nerves went wild, and I did not know what to do. I quickly tried to grab my paddle and my leash, but it was useless. Everything fell into the sea. From one moment to the next I could not balance myself anymore and I fell. In the impetuous fall into the water, I managed to reach an unstoppable speed towards the depths of the sea. I used all my strength to try to stop, but it was impossible. I felt that the sea swallowed me and I in turn swallowed the sea.

I do not know how long the descent lasted, but it was the longest seconds of my life.

Suddenly my body began to stop from that stormy descent. In my heart I could only cry out to God, think about my daughter, my life and desperately sought peace.

I gave up fighting to stop and my body only slowly started to rise. Seeing that it was possible, I began to help myself with my arms. I was trying to stay calm, but I felt like I was going to explode. I reached for the lost surface, not knowing where it was, nor where that giant animal was.

Terror had gripped me. Not being a good swimmer is something I should never have accepted. I tried to calm down, tried to swim anywhere, but my sense of direction was lost. I thought: "I am lost in the sea, I don't touch the bottom, I don't know how deep it is. No one will be able to hear me." I was in the center of the sea. I did not know where my board was, or the paddle, nothing.

I no longer had the strength. I was trying to stay afloat, but I did not know how long I was going to hold out. Breathing did not help me, I was nervous.

-I am going to die. - I was crying and at the same time trying to calm myself to survive.

- I did not come to die here. I cannot believe it. –

My thoughts were so many. My pain was sharp, hopelessness washed over me. I was not able to survive. I was just crying out.

-God help me. -I felt the darkness fall on me. Destructive thoughts began to flow. "I am so ignorant. How could I think that something good was going to happen to me? I should have known that things were going to end badly. God has never been with you. He got you into this problem. You were crazy thinking that He spoke to you and that He loves you. Why is God going to love you?"

And in the middle of my inner battle my voice came out and cried:

-God! God! God! -I was crying inconsolably. It is not possible that like my dad, the sea will swallow me.

-"You can't leave me, God, I have so much to do, Lord, help me." I screamed in torment. I was not trying to make someone listen to my voice, but God to hear me; God have compassion on me and perform a miracle. I thought about his arm, maybe I saw it to have faith. God can come to rescue me with his arm of power. I cried out to heaven for help, for divine intervention, and each breath seemed like an eternity.

I was drowning. My legs had nothing to give any more, my arms neither could help me.

- God, have mercy on me, on my daughter, do not do it for me, I do not want the same thing to happen to her as to me.

- I had so much to do, God. - I was crying in pain. Of disappointment about me, about life, about

God. But faith re-emerged and I was ashamed of my weakness. With all that God has shown me, I cannot doubt. If this is my last day, I just must face it.

Finished. Death seemed to haunt me, and it was a matter of time or an animal bite. I do not know what would be worse. This was not how I wanted to die. This was not the end I wanted. I did not come to Aruba to die. But I gave up. There is nothing more I can do. If you cannot help me, Lord, I understand. Please receive me today in your kingdom. Thank you, my beloved God, for teaching me your infinite love. I want to live with you for eternity in that palace that you showed me. You have been my board of salvation. Take me in your arms and give comfort to my family.

I am sure that was the prayer of my father that day that the sea also swallowed him up. -Everything is cloudy, but my heart is clear. Today is the end, and it is fine. I guess my assignment was somehow complete. I am going with you, Father. We have so much to talk about. It will be beautiful to see you, Jesus. -Those were my words of comfort towards the new season that I had already assumed I was going to live through. Everything continued to become dark and cloudy. There was still light from heaven, but I was not able to discern what my eyes were seeing. My mind was losing clarity. My eyes were losing vision.

When suddenly I began to discern a silhouette, something approached me. There was a light and on that light the silhouette of a man; it was without a doubt the silhouette of Jesus. I knew it was Him who was coming for my life. Joy filled my heart, but I knew it was time for my death. I had joy and peace, but I still felt pain. Why am I leaving, Lord? I knew that by opening my eyes I would be in a beautiful place and I could hug my Daddy again.

Peace increased like a balm; the pain is gone. The silhouette of Jesus was getting closer, as if walking on water. I remembered the passage when He approached the disciples walking on the water and they believed that it was a ghost. "This is what they saw, whoa! what a privilege," I thought. I can see his hair, his long beautiful beard. Slim as I saw him in movies. I am seeing Jesus coming. Peace overwhelmed me in these last moments. As he got closer, my heart was fainting. I heard his sweet voice, but I did not understand him:

- Vengo per te, resisti a una ragazza carina -.

I thought: "They must be angelic languages. Could it be that I already died, and I am in heaven?" The silhouette of Jesus before me melted my soul. Wow, will this be another vision of mine? What an emotion, I am seeing Jesus! Have I started hallucinating?" I wondered.

But wait, does Jesus come on a paddle board? Am I going crazy? - "Sono venuto per salvarti, ragazza mia" (translated into English would be: "I have come to save you, my girl") - He dropped to his knees and placing his arm in the water he took me by my side and he carried me up on to his board. I did not have the strength to help myself up. I was exhausted, totally confused. I felt worn out, I was coughing nonstop, I had swallowed enough water. I was short of breath. A mixture of emotions overwhelmed me. He was just looking at me. On our knees, both on the board, I only heard him say: "Easy, you're safe", with a strong accent that I could not decipher.

A cry from deep in my soul started to come out, and I began to realize that I am alive. My mind is still in total confusion. My crying screams began to come out. They are screams of life, of gratitude, of shock.

-You saved me, Lord! You saved me one more time! You have taken my soul from Sheol! You saved me, God! You came looking for me!

- I could not stop screaming. I have never experienced terror like today, and I am alive because God saved me. I still do not understand what is happening or who this man is, but my heart is pouring out before the presence of God because there is no doubt: He saved me, God saved me.

During my catharsis of thanks to the Lord, I look to see who he is. I still do not know if he is God. I look him straight in his eyes, I am waiting to see my Lord, when the voice of God responding said to me:

-It is him. - And it was so clear to me, almost audible, that I answered loudly:

-Him who? - And the man when he heard me said:

- Oh, I am Donato, I speak little Spanglish.

-Donato? - I asked. He nodded his head and smiled. I foolishly replied - I thought you were Jesus. Hearing myself made me feel so silly. He started to laugh tenderly, just like me. – quanto sono privilegiato - he replied. It was a moment as embarrassing as it was funny. Overly sweet at the same time.

At our language communication barrier, we made ourselves understand and he asked me if I was ready to go back to shore. I answered him after a big sigh: -I am ready to return to life. - We both smiled.

He asked me to go to the front of the board to have better balance, and he started paddling while kneeling. The breeze on my hair seemed like a caress from God. I still could not believe I was alive. I was smiling non-stop, God brought me back to life. My life was never going to be the same again.

-It is him ... What did you want to tell me, God? - I asked God inside me, but there was no answer, just peace. I began to sing a song that flowed like a river from inside me: "I called, you answered, and you came to my rescue, I want to be where you are."* Donato seemed to recognize it and intoned it with me. A peace that passes my understanding is upon me.

We reached the shore and he helped me sit up. Seeing me weak even from the horrible journey, he took me in his arms, carried me to the sand and placed me on a towel. Many people approached. Apparently, they had seen me; some saw what happened. God is so good, that he allowed witnesses and sent for my rescue. How good is God! People start to crowd around and ask me how I feel. I tried not to lose sight

---

*. "Came to my rescue" from Hillsong United.

of my rescuer. I still think that maybe it is an angel and it can disappear. I need to know if that is Jesus.

A few minutes pass, they bring me water, food, and towels to cover myself. I felt like in the vision of the palace, everyone was taking care of me and he is there, his presence a few meters away, in silence, watching, silent, smiling. Like that of Jesus in the palace. This all seems so unreal to me. I keep thinking: "Is it Jesus?"

As if he could imagine what I was thinking, he comes up to me and says to me in his Spanglish-Italian -I promise Yo Donato. - His name, Donato, which means "given by God", his eyes are exceedingly small and pure brown. His gaze reflects peace, serenity, and comfort. He was human, he was not an angel, he was not Jesus. It was real. I looked like a girl watching him, trying to guess. Between laughter, crying and gratitude. He asked me: - May I pray? I am grateful to God for allowing me to save your life signorina, Gesù ti ha salvato, alleluia, I need to adore. - And I, at once started crying. There is no doubt, this is your son, God. It will not be Jesus, but it was given by you to save me from death.

We both immersed ourselves in a prayer of gratitude and worship that lasted the full sunset. When we opened our eyes, everything was dark and there was no one left on the beach: just him and me. And the voice of the Lord again ... - He is. - I did not ask questions.

- io sono italiano - the conversation began. But I am learning English and Spanish. - How cute! - I thought. I had no words to express the emotion that my heart felt." I thought I was going to die, and you came," I said. And he answered: - I am only a servant of God; I only did what He would do. He had me to come on a vacation to Aruba to save a linda signorina from drowning.

-I am also on vacation. Where do you live? - I asked. -I live in Miami. - My heart jumped. Calm down, Pamela, regain control. See that you have swallowed a lot of water and are stunned. Perhaps this is all a vision. - That was the conversation inside me.

Donato has a special sweetness, his treatment is soft, like Jesus. Lives in Miami; this is a lot for my self-control. I was nervous. We talked for long hours and what he said surprised me. Donato is a widower with two daughters, 15 and 14 years old. After the death of his wife, he moved to Miami to start a new life. He told me that he came to Aruba because he felt that he needed time alone with God on the 5th anniversary of the passing of his wife. He had spent a lot of time taking care of his daughters, and he needed time to listen to God's direction.

Five years ago, I came to Aruba to recover from the divorce while he was experiencing the death of his wife and went to Miami. We did not meet in Miami, and we both practiced paddle board, God sent us on vacation to Aruba with the promise of giving us direction and here we met, in such a situation ... I try to contain my emotions and my imagination. Too many matches together. Could it be him?

What I learned today ... So much!

- I learned that in facing fear I will find opposition to become more frightened.
- I understood that there is no fear of suffering. Rather we must fear not to live as slaves of fear.
- I understood that although falls hurt, anticipation makes you think that pain has more power than your own experience.
- I learned that no matter how comfortable and peaceful I feel in life, I should never go unprotected.
- I also learned that what life or the enemy sends you for destruction, God can transform into a blessing.
- I learned that after a terrible fall, rescue can be .... a new story that will begin ...

And remember, if these teachings impart a blessing to your life, share them with others, on your social networks under #Myboardofsalvation

 SHARE

Epilogue

In this adventure I have learned so many things, but I want to share two with you:
    First:

The 20 golden rules for living the paddleboard experience

1- Listen carefully to the coach's instructions. Pause your thoughts, open your ears and your understanding, and learn. Only when we humbly listen and receive instructions from an expert can we be prepared.

2- Measure the extension of your arm with the paddle. There is a paddle suitable for you, for your height. Do not settle for less, do not look for something outside your reality either. Expect the right one, the one that is exactly right for you.

3- Start on your knees. Do not be in a hurry for others to see you on the runway. Your time will come. Meanwhile, your knees are the best place of preparation.

4- Stand without hesitation. When the moment is propitious and you have the "go ahead" of your coach, do not fear, trust, and stand up with determination. Go safe knowing that you are ready for the next step.

5- Stay in the center of the board and take care of the balance. Not in front, not behind. There is a place for you on that board, occupy it and do not move from there. You do not have to play around and go to the front, nor do you have to be left behind. You must be centered.

6- If you are going to fall, drop to your knees. The only way to avoid a fall is on your knees. Without thinking, jump into prayer. During uncertainty, doubt, the mere possibility of falling, your knees will take you to safety.

7- If you fall, take off your life jacket to push yourself up. Pride can lead us to want to demonstrate independence and lack of vulnerability. Remove everything that prevents your climb, leave pride behind, and use everything you got to reunite with your board.

8- If your arms do not help you, use your legs. What works for others, maybe not work for you. Know yourself and use your areas of strength to help you. Do not get frustrated because your strength may be where others lack it.

9- Do not fight with the sea. Flow with situations, adapt to what you cannot control, surrender to what is beyond you and let God fight your battles. It is not your battle; God is in control.

10- To advance, seek to deepen. There is no way you can get to your destination faster if it is not deepening your relationship with God. Spend time in the Word, fasting, and prayer; that will give you the depth to accelerate your victory.

11- To stop, enter the paddle firmly and vertically. There are times when you will need to stop. Stand firm and show your integrity. Do not negotiate your values, or what you have believed in. Just like your paddle, stay upright.

12- Take time to rest. Not everything can be work. Take time to rest and appreciate the Father's love by resting at his feet. Let yourself be loved, let yourself be caressed by the sea of His mercy.

13- Enjoy the ride. Connect with God, listen to his sweet voice, get excited with His words, and celebrate your salvation. This is your time.

14- Contemplate your environment. Look at every detail that the Lord built for you. Observe its beauty in the nature that He gave us. Every day is a new experience of love.

15- Do not look back. When you look back you lose balance and put your destiny at risk. What is left behind, let it go. There are new landscapes to discover.

16- Never take off the "leash". Do not depend on your own prudence. Be humble by learning from His Word daily. Put your trust in God and do not disconnect from the source of your security.

17- Avoid getting too close to extremes. When you get too close to the banks you expose yourself to danger. Stay focused, away from the dangers and the darkness that lurks.

18- Do not go out alone at sea. This tour is more enjoyable in company. Do not feel so spiritual that you do not need anyone. A friend is always good company. Do not expose yourself.

19- Let people know where you are going to be. Always be accountable to someone, for your own safety. Always have someone in your life who knows where and how you are.

20- Do not lose your paddle. Your paddle in this life is the Word of God. You cannot move your board without it. You cannot go on without the instruction manual that He left us.

Bonus- Learn to swim. You can go paddle boarding without having learned, but I do not recommend it. We must prepare for beyond what seems obvious. We must be ready for any eventuality. You never know when you might need it. Learn everything you can. One day you may find yourself on challenging ground where you will have to defend your faith. You do not want to be at a disadvantage that can be fatal. My people perish for lack of knowledge.

Second:

There is no power greater than the power of love

I can testify that I finally met true love. At the end of these five years, the best thing I have been able to achieve has been to fall in love. Yes, I fell in love.

I fell in love with the love of God that filled my world with color and new dreams. I fell in love with his Holy Spirit who, day after day, while guiding me, also conquered me. I fell in love with Jesus, my Lord, and my Savior. And from the day I met that true love, all my gaps were filled. Whether or not Donato is the person God has for me, we will truly find out later. But today I feel full and I have learned to live with an overwhelming love that no man could achieve in me.

That great love is also available to you. My friend, God has a proposal of love for you. Pray this prayer with me and receive the most beautiful gift the world has ever known: the gift of your salvation and living connected to the main and only source of love.

"Lord Jesus, I come to you today with a humble and contrite heart. Forgive my sins, my beloved Lord. I confess that I have failed you. I ask you to come into my heart and wash me of all my evil. Only you can forgive my sin. I recognize you, Jesus, as my only and exclusive Lord and Savior. Write my name in

the Book of Life. I want to do your will and let your Holy Spirit direct my steps. Be my Father and my redeemer. Renew me and create in me a new heart. In the name of Jesus, amen."

If you have made this prayer, I want you to know that right now there is a party in heaven in your name. And I also want to celebrate you.

Send me an email at mitabladesalvacion@ gmail.com because I want to pray for you and stay connected with you.

Enjoy MY BOARD OF SALVATION!

About the author

With My Salvation Board, Elsa iLardo begins her career as an author and novelist, followed by a recognized career as a marketing expert in various industries, including the Hispanic literary industry. Prior to her first book, Elsa has stood out since 2013 as the writer of her blog Mi tabla de salvación, which has tens of thousands of followers.

She is a visionary woman with postgraduate studies in advertising and marketing, she founded and manages, with her husband, Stephen iLardo, the Hispanos Media platform, which has achieved record growth less than a year after its creation. Hispanos Media brings together Hispanic entrepreneurs and professionals residing in Central Florida, with the aim of promoting their development, improvement, and professional exchange.

Along with her professional interests, Elsa expresses her passion for God through an active ministerial life at Lake Mary Church, the church where she and her family gather. She is the leader of a group of Latina women sharing biblical teachings and oversees translations for Hispanic people. Along with her husband, Stephen, they serve as a mentor couple for the youth group and participate in panels on couples' issues. Together they share their testimonies by preaching as guests at events and activities, both in ecclesial and secular organizations. They have traveled to various Hispanic countries as missionaries and serve as volunteers for the ministry of evangelist Chris Franz in crusades and evangelistic events.

Stephen and Elsa iLardo reside in Central Florida, and together they are the parents of Dylan, Cody, and Austin.

Contact information:

@ Email: mitabladesalvacion@gmail.com

Facebook and Instagram: Mitabladesalvación

Facebook and Instagram of the author: elsailardo

StephenandElsa